Nenthrate

---AND---
THE WAR OF HOPE

NENTHRATE UNLEASHING DESTINY, IGNITING HOPE
- THE WAR OF HOPE CHRONICLES

Jaih S Narang

BLUEROSE PUBLISHERS
India | U.K.

Copyright © Jaih S Narang 2023

All rights reserved by author. No part of this publication may be reproduced, stored in a retrieval system or transmitted in any form or by any means, electronic, mechanical, photocopying, recording or otherwise, without the prior permission of the author. Although every precaution has been taken to verify the accuracy of the information contained herein, the publisher assume no responsibility for any errors or omissions. No liability is assumed for damages that may result from the use of information contained within.

BlueRose Publishers takes no responsibility for any damages, losses, or liabilities that may arise from the use or misuse of the information, products, or services provided in this publication.

For permissions requests or inquiries regarding this publication, please contact:

BLUEROSE PUBLISHERS
www.BlueRoseONE.com
info@bluerosepublishers.com
+91 8882 898 898
+4407342408967

ISBN: 978-93-93384-44-7

Cover design: Muskan Sachdeva
Typesetting: Rohit

First Edition: July 2023

My debut book is dedicated to

Jyot, my brother - my hero !

Nani, who nourished me on a diet of books till the time

I could write one of my own!

Be it a word of acknowledgment, a note of appreciation or a piece of advice... Your feedforward is my fuel !
I wait at

narangjaih@gmail.com

About the Author

9 year old Jaih is a multi-talented and highly gifted child. His caliber, competence and creativity are evident in his wizardry with words. The depth of his perception and extraordinary memory leave us stumped on many occasions.

A ravenous reader, he has not only read (and re-read) but also fully comprehended and assimilated the essence of hundreds of books! A music aficionado, he has learned to play the piano on his own and is part of the Pathways School (Gurgaon) choir. He has recently been selected the 'Scholastic Captain' for the Primary School, Student Council 2023-24.

He enjoys playing table tennis and football with equal interest. He regularly notches up top scores in Spelling Bee contests & English Olympiads.

That he has written this amazing book before entering double digits in age, is a feat in itself!

The special influences in my life...

Mom & Dad : the two pillars of my foundation
Dadi : who taught me the art of perseverance
Dadu & Nanu : with their invaluable life lessons
Sumaair : my brave Nenthrate
Pathways School : my second family
Devdutt Patnaik : his unique mythological story telling ignited my creative fire
Amish Tripathi : whose Shiva Trilogy acted as the catalyst for me to put pen to paper

Techno's acting a little strange, it's like something's worrying her. Should I ask? I do not know if she might think that I am hinting at some weakness in her. It would be better if I gathered some more information first. But why would she think that? Let me hope that this question gets answered soon enough. Right now, we've got to go to another planet.

Wait a minute...

That doesn't fit in!

You know what? I think that we should go back to the beginning.

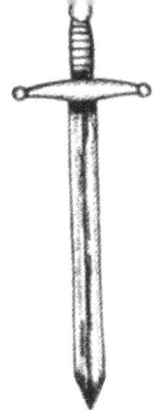

Contents

Nenthrate's goal 1
16 years later 5
The great escape 8
Reunited 20
The strange planet 30
The convoy's war preps 43
The war begins 63
True Path 74
Time to fight 83
Voided 97
The final battle 106

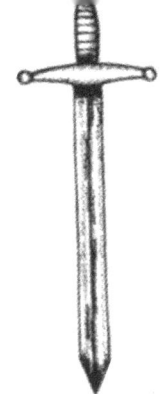

Nenthrate's goal

Nenthrate stood on the rubble, thinking about the war that had been fought. Many destroyed many, and yet evil still remained. The God of Evil had tried to destroy him and his family when he was just a 9- year- old. He did not succeed however, but his father and mother got teleported into different dimensions of the universe. Being at a loose end, what he did most of the time was gather remains of destroyed warriors, both good and evil, and practise fighting with his legendary blade.

Nenthrate knew that somewhere, The God of Evil was raising an army, and that Nenthrate himself was

Good's only hope. The legendary planet of Entaros had been destroyed. However, the one wonderful thing his father had left him as a gift, was the last Sapparator that existed. A sapparator is a device that allows you to transform into different types of aliens, none of which really existed, but were just creations of alien minds. It was to be used only in case of emergencies, like a war scenario, as Sapparators were extremely powerful and could cause mass destruction. His mother had left him a rocket. A strange thing for her to leave him, but it could be very useful now, to embark upon a search for his parents. He knew that they were somewhere in the Seleste universe and the fuel was unlimited. But it was beyond him to strategize how he could search an entire universe. That was a question that was on his mind since forever. He did not want to use the rocket unless he was absolutely convinced about the trajectory he needed to follow to accomplish this mission.

His ally in the mission would be Sarparin, his closest friend, who had survived the explosion too. But the same blast had killed Sarparin's parents and resulted in the mysterious vanishing of Nenthrate's parents and The God of Evil himself. Sarparin was thus left an orphan but he found a brother in

Nenthrate's goal

Nenthrate. They were both confused why only his father, mother and the God of Evil, but not they both had been teleported. Why did this happen? Was this their destiny?

Questions like these floated in their minds constantly. They had walked onto the rocket backwards for the umpteenth time this week. The controls were highly complicated, but they kept practising for more than a month without giving up and soon it became child's play for them. The orange control shaped like a rectangle boosts you just in case an emergency strikes. The biggest control shaped like a circle shoots the Death Bomb, which is feared by all (yes, it's potential is well known all over the galaxy). You can choose the exploding range (maximum 15 planets devastation) and it devastates that area by inflicting 100 % damage. Many of these bombs were used in the Great War which was responsible for taking many lives. It was a long- lasting war with the use of some of the heaviest artillery that ever existed- the powerhouse automatic reload gun, the mega bomb, and the killer weapon- the Colossal Crab, the knight Solgalata's pet. The Colossal Crab had battled Severatol, the 100-headed-devil, who was a loyal servant of The God of Evil. The deadly Severatol died in the war as he was killed by the legendary

Sopramino who was Nenthrate's father's faithful commander in chief.

As Nenthrate got lost in thoughts of the past, he realised at the same time that everything had just started.

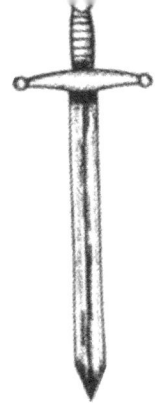

16 years later...

Nenthrate sat on the Elemnolga throne with Sarparin thinking about where the rest of the family might be. Yes, there were more. There was a whole bunch of them. Blados, Techno, and many more. The others took refuge on a strange planet. They wanted to take him too. Unfortunately, he was separated from the rest of the family as the beast Sorpon came in his way while he was running to the evacuation area. After he destroyed him, he came to find the ship gone and he knew there was nothing that he could do about that. It was a tragic loss, and the utter sadness that he was experiencing did not allow him to do much more than disinterestedly explore the land. When the war ended, he had lost almost everything- his land, his family, and his home, yet all was not lost- his loyal friend Sarparin was still with him. Now, they lived in the wrecks and ruins of everything, roaming like free animals on what was left of this gigantic planet.

However, his 25-year-old self was not a quarter as happy and cheerful as his 9-year-old self, due to his losses throughout the war. He had set up an exercise course to keep them fit and ready for the next battle... going around his massive home 10 times, destroying 100 statues (they were already half- broken) and dueling with his friend, which was his favourite and cheered him up no end. He battled hard, but ultimately, both would get knocked out. He liked to transform into Zapparos with the help of his Sapparator. He also liked to take his rocket for a spin and do killer dives into the acidic liquid there (don't worry, it won't harm them because they are aliens) and have a fight with the black crab waiting deep inside. The real terror was the deadly shark called Serantosack (scientific name lumerostaron) reputed to be unbelievably fast and agile. While Serantosack was chasing them mercilessly, Nenthrate's over – the – top - deadly rocket zoomed away, out of Serantosack's reach and when they got back on land, they heaved a sigh of relief to have made the escape from its jaws.

Life was not easy. They were just two people on a completely deserted planet. They finally decided to make good use of the rocket. They were soon drifting off into deep space, searching for a proper, decent planet that would accept them as their own. They travelled to gigantic planets and to planets that could barely hold 100 or 200 ships. They seemed a little too small to be called planets and were of no use to them at all. They finally homed into a giant planet but were amazed and awestruck to find that it was made of fluff. *Fluff!* They made a beeline for the nearest candy store and found strange sweets, like ice-cream caramel lollipops. Umm… said the hungry Nenthrate and they both relished the large variety of eatables available. They went wandering down the paths to survey the surroundings and suddenly after almost 2 hours of aimless walking, they saw a sign made of candy and highly amused, they read it.

It said- Robbers escaped from prison and are on the loose. Any sight of them should be reported to the local authorities or police for capture. Please be safe and have a happy day!

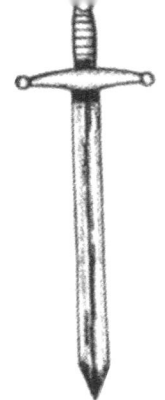

The great escape

They asked a candy man where they could get a map of the city and he said, "I've got an old one around…" He was rummaging through an old box labelled 'Not needed- give- away- stuff.' It was 6:00 by now and it was getting late. They didn't see anybody outside. They were getting a little panicky as they still had to build a home out of the materials they could find but it seemed rude to walk out on the sweet, old man who was trying his best to help them so they waited there. After 30 minutes or so the old man said, "Thanks for waiting!" He gave them the old, dilapidated map and went off to bed. "Sweet old man!" Nenthrate said to Sarparin as they walked off into the distance. And at that very moment, to their horror, they saw the escaped convicts with the chief in the lead.

As soon as the robbers spotted the duo, they started running after them, trying to scare them by waving their thick, muscular arms. However, Nenthrate and Sarparin were not the types to walk away from a good fight so they decided to give them tough competition. The entire town woke up because of all this commotion and came down to see the incident. They battled hard and strong, but the gang of thieves came on them with equal force. Nenthrate had no choice but to engage with them with his Sapparator. He looked for a place to hide and he saw a small, dark alley on some street named Salaphino Road. It was his only hope. Nenthrate ran over to the second alley, on Salaphino Road, sprinting away from the thieves. The thieves saw him and closed in on him. He took out his sapparator and kept saying, "please, please, please turn me into one of my electric guys!" Instantly, he turned into Zapardos. He used his Electric Slash to knock out the thieves.

The others in town arrived when he retreated to Cherry Street after the battle. The crowd saw the thieves knocked out and ran home to fetch their cameras. The news reporters were swarming around him asking all kinds of questions like: "How did you defeat these massive thieves, Will you show me how to operate this strange device?" and many more. Nenthrate emerged as a hero after this intense battle. He had given the Candy Planet the hope that evil could be destroyed, whatever shape it came in.

By now, they were quite exhausted and ready to rest and rejuvenate. A home of their own and a cozy bed was their only desire. Nenthrate was a doer and immediately set out to construct a home according to his mental blueprint. The people watched, and soon, one by one, they came forward to offer all kinds of help. They scattered in different direction to gather all kinds of local materials. Within a few hours, the house stood there as if by magic. By now, everybody was tired and went off to their respective homes. As soon as Nenthrate and Sarparin's heads touched the pillows, they were lost to the world. The next morning, their stomachs rumbling crazily, they set out and ate food just as crazily mixed up. The main diet was lollipops of various hues, sizes and flavours with none of the nutrients which these two were used to. Water here was obtained by melting cotton candy. It tasted unusually foul and their initial excitement of landing on this planet evaporated. They could see clearly that they could not subsist on this monotonous, unusual and unhealthy diet day after day. They were not willing to give up their newly built house but inedible food and unpotable water were serious problems that they could not resolve on a foreign planet. So, with a heavy heart, they decided to move ahead and locate a more conducive planet where they could rethink, recreate and reconstruct the fundamentals of a strong and effective army that could counter The God of Evil.

They again set out on a sojourn through the universe until they spotted a seemingly untouched planet. Sure enough, there were no signs of life when they landed there. It was clearly a just - born planet. By a happy coincidence, there were trees, plants, food and water that matched the diet on their home planet. They were exhilarated. That was it!

They located a large clearing and started building a massive house out of the natural materials that were easily available. They took a shovel and dug up a pool to hold water which would be required for the construction and could later on be used to collect rainwater (water harvesting of today !) They sat upon their floaties inside the pool, sweating because of all the hard work they had done. In no time, they adapted to the new environment and were quite content.

Meanwhile...

The God of Evil had successfully located Nenthrate's home planet; Entaros. More malevolent and powerful than ever before (even though that seemed hardly possible), he had regained his dominance, eagerly awaiting a face to face encounter with Nenthrate. Upon learning of Nenthrate's mysterious disappearence, he let out a resounding scream, his desire to destroy Nenthrate reached new heights! His fury was so intense that it reduced dust and rubble to ashes. His once formidable army had vanished, leaving him wih the urgent task of assembling a fresh and formidable force to once again engage Nenthrate in battle.

Meanwhile, Sarparin urged Nenthrate to hasten their progress while crafting armour for both of them. " Come on, let's pick up the pace!" Sarparin exclaimed. "Do you want to finish this task or not?" Reluctantly, Nenthrate joined in. It had been a while since he had practiced combat since their departure from Entaros. Once the armour was complete, Nenthrate gathered a significant amount of wood, placing it on the rugged terrain of the new planet He meticulously cut the wood into various lengths, organising them into distinct groups, based on their dimensions. The stack consisted of 42 - inch wood pieces, alongside 14.3 – foot and 16.9 foot lengths, with the latter being the largest and the heaviest.

With the wood prepared, Nenthrate embarked on the construction of a training ground. He meticulously laid out an array of intricate traps, dueling areas, and complex obstacle courses- a complete setup for a gruelling training regimen. Nenthrate exerted himself more than Sarparin, as he had built the training ground single-handedly and tested it out by engaging in various exercises. Sarparin, on the other had, lazily stood on the sidelines, offering sporadic words of encouragement without lifting a finger to contribute to the construction. Nenthrate lovingly patted the field, as if it were a cherished pet, satisfied with the result of his efforts.

Then, he decided to go back home, which was right next to the training field. They had just settled in on the couch when a loud noise came at the door. They looked out the window, surprised at the sudden noise as, they had not come across any living creatures while outside. Nenthrate looked out and said, "He seems like some postman." Sarparin said, "Why would a postman knock on the door so loudly?" They pushed the door open and sure enough, they saw a lad carrying a red and white coloured box which was rather big. He looked quite young, wearing multicoloured pants and a shirt which looked like it had been on him for years. He opened the box and said, "Hiya fellows, I'm a postman. My name's Consnitchel Goofyworks Sectaria Entrapran Seletos." "But my friends call me Snitchel." "So, here is your mail." On the mail, it was written - From the God of Evil to Nenthrate. Nenthrate was shell shocked and in a voice that bore resemblance to that of Mickey Mouse (out of shock and not fear), he said, "The God of Evil?" "I knew it. He had survived my blast." His hand shook while he opened the letter which had come as a bolt from the blue. The letter said:

Nenthrate,

You must be surprised that I am still alive. You survived my terrible blast and I barely survived yours. Well, let me get to the point now. Now, I want you to know that I have strengthened my powers greatly. You won't be able to hide now, because I'll carry out a search for you across the Multiverse if I have to till I find and destroy you. Now, listen to me boy, I have raised an ultra-powerful army and you are on your own with no one to help you. I'll find you soon, and fight you to your death. So be warned and be prepared!!

Your mightiest and meanest adversary,

The God of Evil.

Sarparin was even more shaken up than Nenthrate. He stammered, "You h- h heard him. He'll s- search the Multiverse for you." Nenthrate knew that Sarparin was right. There was no hope without an army that could counter The God of Evil's might. Although, raising an army was no joke, in the absence of one, all would be lost. Nenthrate was deep in thought. Suddenly, he stood up. His mind was made. He was determined to destroy The God of Evil "We're raising an army," he announced to Sarparin. " And we're starting the process within the hour." "Bu- Sarparin tried to say. "No buts!" interrupted Nenthrate angrily. His voice shook no more, his nervousness vanished, and he returned to his daring, deadly and determined self. "You heard The God of Evil. He'll search the Multiverse if he has to. We have to make serious preparations to meet the enemy head-on. If he finds us before we are absolutely battle-ready, then we're dead meat."

In another universe...

For a long time, Nenthrate's dad had been in Dome City, stuck in the teleholes. He kept teleporting from one place to another. He remembered Nenthrate with a deep sigh, as he went through the magical void of time and space, waiting to reach his destination. He presumed that his son was already dead, destroyed by The God of Evil's hand. But of course he was wrong. He had been teleporting at random, not knowing exactly where he was heading. Somehow, he had felt strangely drawn to land on this new planet. At first, he shivered at the eerie silence of this new world. But the lush green trees all around and the soothing contours of the place eased his apprehension. He slowly viewed the scene all around... wait a minute, was that a narrow pathway ahead? A path would surely be leading someplace. He followed the mysterious pathway, not imagining in his wildest dreams that it would lead him to Nenthrate. *Who could be living here?* he thought. A training gym too? No animal could use a training gym. He slowly made his way through the narrow, winding lane, finally reaching a house that stood adjacent to the gym and thought he saw a somewhat familiar face at the window.

He drew his powerful sword, prepared for any potential threat and hastened to the house. With his sword raised, he knocked on the door forcefully. Almost instanly the door opened at once. In that moment, father and son stood face to face after years of separation. Nenthrate could not believe his eyes. Was it a mere illusion? He closed his eyes, rubbed them repeatedly, and stood there rooted to the ground. When he reopened his eyes, he was astounded to see his father standing before him. It took him a while to find his voice and in a tearful hushed tone he uttered a single word- "Father". Overwhelmed with emotion, his father embraced Nenthrate, both their hearts filled with disbelief and joy at their miraculous reunion.

It was a deeply emotional and thrilling experience for the long-separated father and son. They spent hours and hours recounting their respective journies and experiences during their time apart. Nenthrate recounted everything he had accomplished during his father's absence while his father narrated the captivating tale of his teleportation across various worlds. It was an exhilarating exchange of thoughts and memories.

Later, Nenthrate proudly led his father to the training ground, explaining that he had single handedly constructed it. They exercised together, reveling in their freedom to push their physical limits. In a mock battle, Nenthrate lost by a few strikes and finally, they went for a walk on the beautiful, mystic, planet. In a way, they were trying to relive their wonderful past on Entaros, the planet they once called home.

At night, they sat inside the blankets making hand shadows and laughing and talking and though both of them were exhausted, sheer excitement kept them awake. Nenthrate then shared with him, his deepest fears about The God of Evil and all the foolproof plans he had been devising to meet the inevitable challenge. He reiterated before his father in clear and determined words, his pledge to annihilate The God of Evil and spread the light of Good and Hope throughout the Multiverse. Gradually, father and son dozed off. A few hours later, Nenthrate's dad sensed something approaching the window. To his horror, it was a gigantic creature looking extremely fierce and deadly. *Oh God*, he thought, *that'll be a tough challenge for Nenthrate and Sarparin.*

Then he remembered that he had given Nenthrate a Sapparator. He called him quickly as the monster was closing in on the house. "No match for me!" declared Nenthrate as he transformed into Atomous and destroyed the monster with his atomic breath. "That'll come in handy in the war!" he said playfully. He and his father laughed along with Sarparin and then went off to sleep...

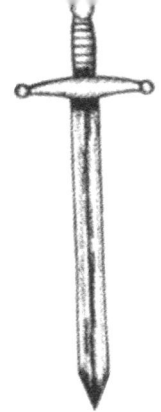

Reunited

It was a comforting feeling to have his father back at his side but their reunion was far from complete. Once again Snitchel appeared, claiming to be enamoured with the design of their home. Before allowing him entry Nenthrate couldn't help but mutter "Okay Consnichel whatever sheepsbutt"- "actually it's Consnichel Goofyworks Sectaria Entrapran Seletos" interrupted Snitchel. Nenthrate, visibly annoyed retorted "Does it matter?!"Has The God of Evil sent you yet again?" He asked with a threatening, terrorising whisper. "N- N- no" Snitchel replied with a look of utmost horror on his face. He knew that he would be accused as a spy.

Aware of the impending accusation Snitchel knew he had no evidence to prove his innocence. "You don't have any proof." Nenthrate said, raising an eyebrow. "I mean, you were with him, otherwise how would you give me the mail from him?" asked Nenthrate. Snitchel was fearfully contemplating the next few words coming out of his mouth. Finally he mustered the courage to speak"The God of Evil entrusted me with his deepest, darkest secrets."

Instantly captivated Nenthrate leaned in, excitement evident in his eyes. "Tell me! Is it the key to his destruction?" he exclaimed unable to contain his anticipation. The words were barely out of his mouth, when he faced a horrifying sight - Snitchel's eyes had turned black. His skin turned as red as a tomato. He was in some sort of a trance. He took out some thing from his pocket.

Out came two shiny, gold swords from his pocket, maneuvering speedily to pierce Nenthrate. A near miss from the heart! He was seriously hurt. Suddenly, a telehole emerged and lo and behold, a strange figure wrapped in a black cloak appeared. The emerald green eyes glimmered even in the weak light that penetrated a few trees of the dense forest. The sword in the entrant's hand was longer than Snitchel's two swords combined. Snitchel's attention turned towards the figure. A fight began. He was more than ready to exterminate the figure if he had to. A near miss from Snitchel's sword forced the cloaked figure to jump backwards. The figure retaliated with such power that Snitchel fled from the scene. The figure removed the cloak and without revealing the face, picked up the badly wounded Nenthrate gently and took him up to the bed. The mysterious figure finally spoke to them.

"Those are bad wounds, but he'll be fine soon." The words brokenly flitted through Nenthrate's mind like an echo from his past, clearing the mystery of the figure. Believe it or not, it was Nenthrate's mother! Recognising her voice, Nenthrate gave a weak moan. Nenthrate's father was incredulous- first Nenthrate, and now his wife- it was too much for him. In his overwhelmed state, he began dancing and jumping wildly on the floor without a care in the world. It was like a dream come true for father and son. Nenthrate soon got better with the caring touch from his mother, father, and friend. As soon as he bounced back, he narrated to his mother, his determined plan of recruiting a big army to counter The God of Evil. His mother was more than willing to join up and help them raise an army, and give the required boost to exterminate The God of Evil who was on a mission to spread evil all through the Multiverse.

It was a few months since they had arrived on this vast planet and everybody wanted to stay for longer, but Nenthrate insisted that they had to move on because, who knows if The God of Evil might be travelling at this very moment to their present location. Snitchel had already carried the warning from The God of Evil that he was on their trail. They finally set out to find a decent planet but alas, ended up brushing a black hole by mistake. Nenthrate pressed the booster. It didn't work. You probably think they were doomed but that was not the case. You see, in a panic Nenthrate pressed the same button again and luckily, the extra boosters came out. They finally got out of the powerful influence of the black hole, but it was a close call. They went at top speed for two whole days, their coordinates at the front of the Seleste universe. The super speed was thrilling but they had a crash with an asteroid soon enough, causing 69% damage to level E- *THE ENGINES*. This resulted in an unexpected crash landing upon a strange planet.

The rocket had landed close to a structure which resembled an immensely large laboratory. The ship had taken a lot of damage and it would take weeks, even months to fix it! They walked around the laboratory, looking for a secret entrance. Sarparin spotted a sword cleverly hidden in the crack of a rock. It seemed only an elf would be able to remove it. The smallest member of the army- Sarparin went ahead to remove the sword. As soon as he removed the sword, an alarm sounded. The sound made them freeze! They were trapped in pods. "Interesting technology!" remarked Nenthrate. Within minutes, scientists with advanced-looking weapons emerged from a tiny opening in the hidden entrance. The leader (so they presumed) said, "Who are you intruders?" with a look of annoyance on her face.

Nenthrate and the others could not fathom the expression.

"Who are you?" said Nenthrate with a look of surprise. The leader strangely looked like his sister, Techno. "I'm Techno Solaris." the leader said. Nenthrate was stunned.

For a few seconds, he was speechless. "I'm Nenthrate S - Solaris." Nenthrate stuttered. Techno gasped! She had a totally mechanical expression on her face, even as she looked at her long lost brother. For Nenthrate, Techno was his long-lost but not long-forgotten sibling but the same could not be said about Techno. Her life had been so enmeshed in advanced technology that she could not feel much emotion anymore. "Long time no see, Techno!" said Nenthrate with a half smile on his face. "What's going on, Nenthrate?" said Techno. "Same as 16 years ago." "No way. How?" said Techno who didn't believe in beating around the bush. "I don't know how he survived, but I do know that he's ready to have a war and he's more powerful than ever now." "You're fighting a losing war against The God of Evil", said Techno. "I know." said Nenthrate. "But we're raising an army to counter them and give them a fight that they will remember." "Don't you wanna join?" asked Nenthrate after a pause, though he already knew the answer. Techno said, "Don't you already know?" He gave Techno a look that said "*Yep!*" Then he said, " You will be a very strong mentor for our army in all technical matters. Today's wars use highly advanced technology and who better than you, Techno, with your brilliant mind which we all appreciated even when you were little baby."

Techno responded matter-of-factly as she bragged,"The process of building these kind of weapons is quite simple.""We just eliminate the chemicals and then activate the…"wait, wait, wait"Nenthrate quickly interjected saying "First of all, I lost you at easy." "Second, I have no idea what you're talking about.

And thirdly, I am no scientist. Clear?" "Yeah, it's nonsense", said Techno sarcastically. "Anyway, let's move to the more important stuff- showing you the rest of the laboratory.

She continued "This is the invention room, and that tall thing is the magritransfier. It can tell us anything we ask it." Nenthrate asked jokingly, "can it tell us the location of an ice cream shop nearby ? I could use something cold!" "Of course", said Techno. She typed something that looked like gibberish. Noises came and the machine emitted noises that sounded like "urkenkoco." A second later, Techno said, "finego ofvil." "Literally sis?" Said Nenthrate. "Finego Ofvil? Is this some alien code?" "No!" laughed Techno. "I'm just requesting some coordinates for The God of evil."

"Techno," said Nenthrate, "you are a genius." "Here," said Techno. "Put these headphones on. You'll understand soon enough." Saying this, Techno smiled in her most appealing way and Nenthrate put them on and listened." "According to my calculations" said the strange robot voice, "the God of evil is trillions and trillions of megametres away from us. He is in the bottom of the Seleste universe." Nenthrate eagerly addressed his companions "Guys did you hear that?" " Maybe, not exactly", said Techno. "Some of the sound is blocked from reaching us. We could only make out, acorcal illion. Most of the sound waves had bounced back."

"What I broadly understood is The God of Evil is pretty far away from us", Nenthrate explained. "This device could really be useful." said Nenthrate. "Even better", said Techno. "We can take the entire laboratory. But you can't go. It hasn't got your print." "No problemo", said Nenthrate. "We have a rocket. We can go together side by side. Go at your maximum speed." "Wait, said Techno. Our maximum speed is trillions of kilometeres per hour." Nenthrate said, "Oh, I think we may be able to match that! *Our* ship moved at an unbelievable speed when we once escaped from a black hole even though we entered its event horizon." "That's good for me", said Techno.

"We should go now," said Nenthrate. "But there is one problem", he showed them the rusted ship. "Ok... that is a problem. Luckily, we've got the enmaterialiser." Within a minute or two, a machine the size of a tall room, about 7 – 8 feet high, appeared and Techno pressed a button while pulling a lever. 'Boom!', went the machine and Nenthrate thought the rocket had exploded but in a minute or two, when the smoke cleared, the machine looked completely new and untouched. *Techno's acting a little strange, it's like something's worrying her. Should I ask? I do not know if she might think that I am hinting at some weakness in her. It would be better if I gathered some more information first. But why would she think that? Let me hope that this question gets answered soon enough. Right now, we've got to go to another planet.* He looked at his rocket. All refurbished, shiny and clean, now more than ever before.

He asked Techno in the ship, "You're acting a little strange. Why, are you worried?" He knew that she was not normal. "It's just that, well, if we lose the war, then it's all over. You—we are dead. So then it'll be a waste- dying for nothing. It's not what I want. If I need to get rid of this feeling, then I'll have to send this fear flying." "Well, I didn't think of that" said Nenthrate sheepishly. "But I assure you, if at all we lose, (which to me is not even a remote possibility) we lose with honour, we die with honour." "Thanks" said Techno, "I really needed that." It seemed that she had snapped out of her mechanical mood to offer true sisterly support.

A few hours later, Snitchel's trance was back. "Where is that guy now?" Nenthrate complained. An alarm blared, "ENGINES LOST! Preparing spare boosters." "Snitchel's work," said Nenthrate, , As soon as he reached the engines, he fell down on to his knees, holding his head. He felt pain rising up his head. He was sweating profusely and in the haze of pain and confusion, he heard a menacing voice. "You are finished," said the familiar voice. He felt dizzy. Enveloped by a fit of trembling, he fainted...

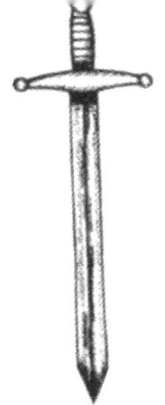

The strange planet

A few days had elapsed. Nenthrate opened his eyes slowly and carefully, but was unable to get up. "What happened?" He said groggily. "We found you in the engines, bleeding severely", said Techno. " Wait, wait, wait. I heard a message from a familiar voice-" Techno cut him off. "Relax for now big bro. You have not completely recovered yet but for your information, Snitchel's fine." Nenthrate went back into deep slumber once again. His sleep was abruptly interrupted by Techno calling out his name excitedly. He jumped from his bed in shock and surprise. It was 2:00 in the morning. "What is it?" Said Nenthrate. "Look", said Techno excitedly. "I have located ample space on a cool - looking planet with a population of approximately 1,00,000! We could combine forces with them!" "I don't think that's a good idea," said Nenthrate. "You see, other planets don't really like aliens, so it could be a wasted trip." "Do you want to win this war or not?" Techno screamed. "You very well know, we have a very powerful, malevolent enemy who will be the destroyer of all good in the universe if not checked and annihilated as soon as possible." Nenthrate was taken aback. He had never seen Techno this infuriated. "OK", he gave in.

The ship flew down to the strange planet. It was Earth itself! It looked primitive from their point of view. They landed on a small area full of rubble. Their ship left a giant crater-like mark on the surface of this mysterious planet. As soon as Nenthrate walked to the door leading to his rocket, it said, "Password?" Nenthrate said "829J1JIH7" and the door opened, but it said "Correct" reluctantly, sighing as if it was more used to intruders than members. This was the cockpit of the ship. His rocket was hidden there. The plan changed when Techno insisted that it was safer if they put it in a more heavily guarded area. He searched around the massive room and at that moment a few bookshelves caught his eye. They looked misplaced in that area so he removed them and strangely, there appeared a few tall thickets of grass behind them.

"What?" said Nenthrate in surprise. He suspected it was double security so he pushed aside the grass and then saw a gate. Some guards were there. Behind the guards a figure stood still. Where was his rocket? He racked his brain, thinking who could it possibly be. Soon, he recognised that this was his old buddy, Radrason. This was no ordinary rocket- It was his friend in disguise. The rocket was more than a gift. It was his companion. Before they could even talk, an alarm blared. "Emergency!", cried Nenthrate. He hurriedly told Radrason to stay there while he rushed to the spot where it had blared. The guards lay there, knocked out. A big hand was there, with a massive body and gigantic muscles. Nenthrate got ready to fight him, all alone.

"Veldos!", screamed The God of Evil. "How is the attack going? I want a success!" "It is going well sir, said Veldos. General Atrimandos is fighting with Nenthrate. He's thrashing him. Watch", he said. A screen which was shaped like a circle was showing Nenthrate falling down in slow motion. "Ha Ha Ha!" Laughed The God of evil. "His misery is my happiness! Those despicable Entarians!" But all of a

The strange planet

sudden, he screamed, "NOOOO!" The general had fallen down to the ground because Nenthrate had used his sapparator to transform into Gigasaurus. Alright! Said Nenthrate, power running through his veins.

"Man, let me transform in to Atomous!" There was a bang and a flash. "Grrrr..." growled General Atrimandos. "X-men, attack!" Within 30 seconds, armoured men appeared. Not just 10, 20, 30, but hundreds of them of them lined the walls. But that was no problem at all! Nenthrate had a few plus points-

1. He was bigger than all of them combined.
2. He really packed a punch with Atomous.
3. They are robots. With the power of $e=mc^2$, he could crush them.

Seriously? Said Nenthrate. "Oh yeah, that's my full power," said General Atrimandos sarcastically. Within 6-7 minutes, General Atrimandos hurt Nenthrate badly while fighting. "Oh boy", said Nenthrate. "Goodbye!" said the general, but Nenthrate had already recovered. "I will destroy you!" promised General Atrimandos. "Don't make promises you can't keep!" Said Nenthrate. "Hiyaaaa!" There was an explosion and the screen went black.

"WHAT HAPPENED?!" Said The God of Evil. Veldos said, "the cosmolo internet is beyond our range. Should I extend it?" "Just do it!" Said The God of Evil. The screen flickered back on. "I've had enough! "Ultimate Energy Blade! Screamed Atrimandos.

"Ooh," said The God of evil. "And I'm supposed to see Nenthrate still alive?" "We may have underestimated that puny Nenthrate's abilities." Veldos replied. "A Sapparator is the source of his great power." Veldos added . The God of Evil was flummoxed "oh for God's sake let us just destroy the sapp- whatever that thing is." he stammered.

"Sapparator, my lord," replied Veldos hastily. The God of Evil looked at him angrily, and instantly he said, "m- my apologies, my lord. " Veldos suddenly said, "Look my lord." The God of Evil looked at the screen. HAHAHA! He cackled madly. Nenthrate was lying on the floor, knocked out by the powerful energy blast. Now to finish you, said General Atrimandos. At that very moment, Radrason came onto the scene. "Deathray Blast!" He cried. "Thanks bro," Nenthrate said calmly. "Now let's finish him like old times," said Nenthrate. General Atrimandos was starting to recover. "Ultimate twosome blast!" They both cried out at the same time.

KRAKABOOM!!! The moment they opened their eyes, the general was gone. They whooped and danced a victory jig.

"Seriously?" Said The God of Evil, annoyed. "We have better generals. General Eslacore could have finished him in seconds!" Veldos said, "but he does not know the location of Nenthrate." "Location, schmocation, I don't care." said The God of Evil. "I want him NOW!" "We shall have him in time," said Veldos calmly.

Those who had been knocked out in the engine-room recovered in 3 days. Nenthrate was thinking about his original planet, Serantosack, and the ruins there. But now was no time to do that. They were going to the humans to ask for their help and win this war. "Nenthrate?!" called out his dad. "Yeah?" said Nenthrate calmly. "C'mon, we're going to the humans!" said his dad. "Are you sure this is a good idea?" said Nenthrate. His father did not answer. He just started walking ahead. Nenthrate ran over to him. They went out of the ship with the others. The city was filled with colour. They went over to the place where there were more humans and got ready to announce their arrival. Everyone was scared, though they tried not to show it.

As soon as they became visible to the humans, the humans started muttering what sounded like "mimblewimble." "Um... excuse me...", said Nenthrate, his voice trailing off, but surprised that he found the courage to do that. "I am Nenthrate. These are my friends. You must be wondering what we are doing here. We have an enemy who is, to put it mildly, Pure Evil Incarnate and is battling with us since long to overpower the complete Multiverese. We want you to join us. Your population can boost our army a lot. I would like to speak to your leader here, please." A thin man with a formal shirt and tie and a scar on his face, signifying that he had been to war, stepped forward. "I am Endren. We do not know of your kind, but a request like that shows that you mean us no harm. If this is going to be a long journey, then we'll have to pack the essentials like food and water first." "No need, said Nenthrate. We have all the essentials on the ship. Step inside", he said warmly. They all went to the ship. Techno and Nenthrate stayed behind , watching them. "Well, that went well," whispered Nenthrate in a funny voice. "Told you so", said Techno, in the same type of voice. Nenthrate laughed.

A week after this incident, Nenthrate went on patrol duty in the ship. They had reached the south of the Seleste universe, a good distance from The God of Evil. Nenthrate had heard about Techno making some new invention. He went to check it out. He gasped when he saw it. A battle weapon called the God Bomb Ultra stood ready to fire. The maximum amount of devastation this weapon could cause was 30 planets! "Nice," said Nenthrate with a smirk which looked like he was up to no good at all.

The sound of human chattering filled the air. Nenthrate had gone to the cafeteria to check on the food for the humans! Techno was searching for him. "What happened?" said Nenthrate when Techno found him. Before Techno could answer, a loud crash and a bang made them turn their heads in the direction of the noise. "BOOM!" "Oh now what?!" said Nenthrate. "Just when we are doing *target practice* a stupid monster ruins our plans! UGGGGH. Wait a minute sis", said Nenthrate, "I'll be right back after demolishing this new general." He transformed into Lightspeed and set off. 2 seconds later, he arrived back. "Yeah, I'm done. Lightspeed's really good, he really moves at the speed of light."

"ARGHHHHHHH!" screamed The God of Evil. "Another General fallen in battle! This stupid- Wait, I have an idea!" He said madly. "Send multiple generals! NOW, do you understand? N O W! I'm saying slowly so that your pathetic little brain can understand. No arguments!" "Clashrem, Speedstrike, Ultisaur, fight!" said Veldos quickly. They emerged and disappeared in a flash. "WHOOOOAAAAAA!!! " They all screamed. Everyone except Speedstrike. "Are you kidding?" he said. "This is good. I could sleep here in this void!" "Hoooowww couuuuuld yoooooooooou thiiiiiiink ooooooooof sleeeepiiing nooooooow?" shrieked Ultisaur. His voice was filled with anger and fear. Suddenly, it stopped and they fell down. They all had landed on the human's planet. "Alright! Let's go wreck some Nenthrate butt!" said Speedstrike.

They went to the area of the first attack, by General Atrimandos, but nothing, just some fire. "Ha! The general burned them all up!" said Speedstrike. "No," said the others. Suddenly, someone appeared and killed Speedstrike in one stroke. He was a heavily armoured man, with black drapes, he was taller as compared to Nenthrate, a sapparator around his forehead, with black eyes and swords of all kinds. Nenthrate was back on the ship, watching this mysterious alien. He gasped. He had a sapparator like him. *Who in the world is this guy? I thought that my sapparator was the last one in existence! My brother used to have a sapparator, but he was destroyed in the war, along with his sapparator. Am I dreaming?* He slapped himself on the face. The man was still there. *No way! I'm going down to check it out.*

He used Techno's new device, the ultramagnator to go down to Earth. He fought alongside him. After the generals retreated, they both said, "Who are you?" "I am Blados, said the cloaked man. "I am Nenthrate", said Nenthrate. "WHAAA?" said Blados. "You're still here?" "Yep," said Nenthrate with a happy sigh. Blados was Nenthrate's brother. You've become stronger, he said with a smile. But The God of Evil has too. We better go back to the ship. "Oh wait," he said. Nenthrate told him all about what had happened till now. At the ship, they were paying attention to nobody but each other. "So this is what's happened?" he confirmed. "These are tough times," said Nenthrate. "Hmm," he said seriously. "What's the matter?" asked Nenthrate. "That's the matter," he said pointing to a new general. General Sesleron. "You know him?" said Nenthrate? "No time." said his brother. "NOW!" He screamed and transformed into Silion. "Let's go!" He said. A horrendous fight took place, with blades and atoms flying everywhere. (Nenthrate transformed into Atomous). They had a fight in the engine room... again. Nenthrate finished General Sesleron faster than any of the other monsters he had fought because of his brother. "Nice!" They yelled in unison. "We won."

"Password?" said the gate. "A S H Y 8 7 7 7" said Blados enthusiastically. "Wrong," the gate said. "Nenthrate! A little help please!" he called out. "1 H J S A 7 8 9 J Y" said Nenthrate. "Done,". The door opened only for them to find a room with another door. "Double Security," he said, and then said "1 Y U I O B." There was another room with 15 doors. The annoying ones, said Nenthrate. Try one, he said. "1 Y I O T U." said Blados. Nope, said Nenthrate. Within seconds, a huge ray appeared and powered up, ready to fire, "1 D H U 8 M G T U J H T Y J N T J U 9 M V F D V X A D N H J K U N M G J J U 8 9 0 1 3 5" said Nenthrate hurriedly and the ray went back into the ceiling. "Thanks for the save," said Blados. A voice behind them said, thanks for being so careless and letting me kill you! Nenthrate looked back. "Strike of destruction!" a new general said, aiming his hand toward Blados. "Blados!" Nenthrate screamed while taking the hit himself, only to feel the free flow of blood down his body. He fell down unconscious. Blados knew Nenthrate was in danger. If he didn't get him back to the Medbay quickly, he would die. "Ultrapick." said Blados. He fought with all he had, dripping in sweat. He used his Sapparator, destroyed Ultrapick but was horrified at the thought that Nenthrate may be dead. If he actually was dead, he would've died for nothing at all. Taking Nenthrate to the Medbay was the most tense moment he could remember till now. Techno said that he was alive but barely. He opened his eyes after almost three weeks. He felt OK, but he couldn't get up. The blast had been very powerful. Nenthrate was surprised he had survived it.

Nenthrate immediately ran over towards the battlefield to find that the war was still on. The screams of people who were dying and the number of fallen bodies was increasing rapidly, filling the air, water and earth, or what was left of it. He joined the fight. He wished he had been taller but being just 9 years old… that wasn't easy. Although he was skilled at fighting, others could thrash him. He fought with the easy enemies. A building fell. He saved himself just in time. He hated the war. He battled hard and strong, but no matter what he did to the strong guys, he had to retreat if he wanted to remain alive. His mother and father were fighting The God of Evil. Suddenly, there was a flash of light and all of them were gone. "NOOOOOO!!!"

Nenthrate was shaken up by this dream. He knew that he had found his parents, but just the memory of that horrific scenario scared him deeply. He prayed that this would not happen again. He was sweating like mad. The memory of that ultimate battle on his home planet horrified him even now. He coughed. *Just forget about it Nenthrate*, he calmed himself.

Tap... Tap... Tap...

At 3:00 in the morning Nenthrate heard this sound. He woke up Blados and told him about the noises. They peeked into the kitchen and saw a new general. This strange general said, "General Corsander will fail." "V4HHUIOo is the code for this door," Nenthrate whispered. "Also, we have heard that a new general is coming. Is that general trying to- Not possible." "Maybe it is possible." Blados replied. "Uh hello general," said Nenthrate. "Huh?" said the general. Are you trying to help us? Nenthrate said. "No... Maybe... Yes."

he said. The message conveyed was just not clear. "I thought that no general would help," said Blados...

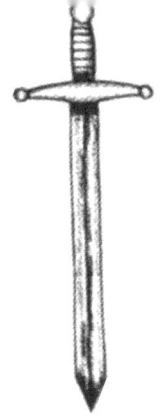

The convoy's war preps

"Let me get this straight," said Nenthrate. "Some general shows up at 3:00 in the morning, is unsure if he's going to help us, and now we're supposed to trust him? Sounds like a bad plan to me!" "But if he's actually with us, we can have the upper hand!" replied Blados. "We can know what The God of Evil is planning, for instance, and also which generals they will send next!" "I'm with you, you know," the general said. "We don't even know you," said Nenthrate skeptically. "I am General Crashpilot. They call me that on the account of the wings," he said showing his wings, "but I like it, because it's cool." "OK, we'll trust you," said Nenthrate "but if you betray us, it is over for you." "I have to go back to my ship to gather more information," explained General Crashpilot. He swiftly bid them goodbye and zoomed away. "Bad enough," said Nenthrate. "We can't trust him." "Maybe, maybe not," said Blados. "You never know!" Nenthrate remained cautious, suggesting "He may be trying to double cross us…", before deciding it was time to rest and heading to bed.

"1 0 7 5 3 H Y U I K L M's the new password, Nenthrate" said Blados. "Ooh, look who's got his own membership card!" Nenthrate remarked. "What type?" he added. "Progressor," replied Blados. "Nice, mine's Premium," said Nenthrate. "Oh, by the way, at Premium we can change passcodes and I just did!" "What?" said Blados in surprise. "N J S N I 9 3 6 S," replied Nenthrate. They both laughed. Nenthrate turned around to find Sarparin next to him. "Hiya there, Sarparin," said Nenthrate. "Been in your quarters for way too long." "Hey! said Sarparin, check this out. A shapeshifter device," he said, showing them.

"I can shapeshift into one of those generals and then go and get information. I can even clone myself." "Watch." "Y 7 H 1 X X D Y." Clone sequence activate," he said calmly. He cloned and de-cloned over and over. "Okay, Okay," said Nenthrate." "Enough." That was cool. This is all you were doing?" "You have no idea how hard it was to make this thing." said Sarparin. "Yep," Nenthrate replied, trying to end the conversation.

"Don't know anything about normal technology, but I know a lot about this!" said Sarparin. "By the way Nenthrate, tomorrow's your human friend's birthday." Nenthrate smiled. At least there was one thing fun he could do when they were in a crisis like this again.

6 hours later:

Nenthrate was reading his favourite book, The Battle of Infinity series, Book 6, the last of the series. He had reached page 277 / 389. It was the part where Bralidite, a brave soldier, sacrificed himself to destroy the Legendary Ulcraminos. He squealed in excitement. "Yo, check this out," said Nenthrate to Techno, Blados and Sarparin. Sarparin was at page 178, Techno was at 239 and Blados at 143. Nenthrate was overwhelmed by the 6th book which had just come ~~in~~ out The Battle of Infinity series and so he was reading at a faster pace than anybody. "Nenthrate..." said Blados. "Let us discover this book ourselves. Do not reveal the secrets, at the very least." "Oh all right!" "Your loss..." said Nenthrate. "The sixth book rocks..."

In the Future:

The God of Evil swooped down along with Nenthrate and Blados towards 'him'. An explosion hit The God of Evil. Nenthrate took out his phone. "Arsicon!" said Future Nenthrate. "Please tell Past Nenthrate about the theory. He's our only hope." Arsicon disappeared.

Well, you can imagine what happened next. Arisicon went into the current timeline that Nenthrate was in. Nenthrate was surprised when Arsicon told him the real reason for his appearance. "Oh, OK. So when I finish the Battle of Infinity series, I'll know that I have been chosen by Sorderastros to destroy The God of Evil." asked Nenthrate. "Well, then I'm actually not such a screw up. I guess," he said with a sigh, getting up. "Hey," said Arisicon. "You are doing well in the future, just FYI." Nenthrate smiled. Good luck, Arsicon . Wait, Nenthrate said, "if you are from the future then how does the battle end?" "Telling you would change time," said Arsicon. "But you'll get to know. Goodbye," he said as he walked back into the portal leading to his timeline... "That was one heck of a story," sighed Nenthrate. "Or one heck of a reality."

The convoy's war preps

He laughed. "Boom!" "What now?" He got up. Just then, Techno and Blados appeared. It's worse than we thought, they both said quickly. "Why are you so bruise—"Come!" interrupted Blados, pulling him roughly. When Nenthrate rushed to the scene, his jaw dropped. The God of Evil HIMSELF...

"What do you want from us?" Nenthrate roared. The God of Evil smirked devilishly. "I'll show you!" In an instant, they were teleported to The God of Evil's ship. Blados and Techno were in a small cage while Nenthrate was free. "What have you done?!" shouted Nenthrate. The God of Evil's plan was already formulated- "Let's have a one on one duel. If I win, I get to destroy your friends and you. If you win, then you can get out of here alive." he said. "A very clever plan indeed, but it's fine by me," said Nenthrate, slowly calming down and determined to rescue his family. "Hiiiiiiyyyyaaaaaaa!!!!!" screamed Nenthrate like never before. The God of Evil ran toward him with his sword. Nenthrate transformed into his most powerful alien- Ultracranos. "I'll destroy you with or without your sapparator," said The God of Evil. The God of Evil hit Nenthrate, while Nenthrate retaliated with equal force. They both let out a cry of pain. Nenthrate hit him again and again. His hits shook the ship. "Boom! BOOM!!!" He held The God of Evil's hand, directing it backwards to hit The God of Evil himself and kept saying, stop hitting yourself, stop hitting yourself, with a mocking laugh.

Finally, The God of Evil said, "Our first battle ends here as it was only a sampler to give you a taste of my wrath and power. I will let you all go now, but I assure you, we will meet again soon, and the war that is to come will be much longer, and much more disastrous, destructive and deadly. Goodbye." Saying this, The God of Evil teleported, Nenthrate, Blados and Techno back to the ship. The God of Evil had left a mark on Nenthrate and it hurt. "You rocked, Nenthrate," said Sarparin when he heard about the incident. "Nice," said Blados. "Butt kicking is your middle name," said Techno. Nenthrate could hardly wait. Tommorow was his birthday when he would move one step further towards the next decade of his life.

"Happy Birthday to you, Happy Birthday to you!"

The birthday songs filled the air as Nenthrate came to the hall of the ship. Everyone was dressed in bright clothes of all sorts. He was really happy that he could actually celebrate in a crisis like this. "Run away," said General Crashpilot, suddenly appearing on the scene. "I knew it," said Nenthrate but that was

The convoy's war preps

just Sarparin and his device. Nenthrate laughed at that one. "Ha Ha Ha! I've changed the code," Nenthrate said. "It's N E N T H R A T E P R O 2 6. It's a specialised code." Game time! They played Sly fox. The dens in that game were Sarparin, Nenthrate, Techno and Blados. Nenthrate accidentaly stubbed his toe while running. I wish you were there at the party. They even had a balloon fight. Finally, it was time for the cake cutting, Nenthrate's favourite part of the celebrations. He rushed to the table to cut the cake. "Happy birthday to you, Happy birthday to you! Happy Birthday, Happy birthday, Happy birthday to you!!!" The humans sang the next part, "May God, bless you." Nenthrate said, "The God of Evil won't bless me." Everyone laughed at that one. It was a wonderful time, people laughing, enjoying and gorging on the delicacies. I remember the time of Nenthrate's birthday till now, it was awesome and I wish you had been there. Back to the main story now...

"Isn't it obvious?" said Nenthrate to the others. "We are going to be a *Clezos (Five United)*. We're four united. We just need to find one more and we'll be complete.

The God of Evil works alone. That's why he can never win. If we work together, then we can destroy him. If we get torn apart, The God of Evil will surely have an advantage.

First things first, we have to keep ourselves from being ripped apart." "You've mentioned that already", interrupted Blados. "Let me speak," said Nenthrate. "Second, keep together, move together and attack together. Third, Be persistent and positive."

The next day, Crashpilot came back to the ship to provide information to Nenthrate and Blados. "General Corsander is coming." he announced "Today?" Nenthrate said, "Oh jeez, come on! Why today?! Today was supposed to be my fun day. I thought no General Corsander or any other of these stupid generals would come. You gotta be kidding me! Seriously? Re-" "I can't control the boss." Crashpilot interrupted Yeah, we know, said Nenthrate. "Besides, General Corsander will kill-" "Yeah, we know," said Nenthrate. "So I'm leaving to get more info." "Wait a minute," said Nenthrate, "you have more to tell us, don't you." "OK, you got me," said General Crashpilot. "The master is about to track your ship." "The engines have been destabilised by Corsander." "Ok, now I've gotta go. If Corsander finds me here he'll kill me." Saying this, he left with a whoosh! "Corsander won't be able to kill Crashpilot

The convoy's war preps

'cause he'll be dead by the time we're through with him." said Nenthrate, with full confidence and a cheeky look on his face.

Let's see how the battle unfolded. It had a touch of humour to it. It was actually a little funny. Nenthrate transformed into Scorpon, gave his Legendary Blade to Blados, and he managed to hit general Corsander on the chest leaving him unable to retaliate. General Corsander was hurt but struck again at Nenthrate, A narrow miss. Nenthrate realised he had to be alert with this General as he was quite powerful. Blados tried to hit General Corsander but the General had already adapted to these tactics. He lunged forward to take the sword but Blados ran away just in the nick of time. Corsander's hand struck the hall wall instead. Blados knew he would have to hit him as hard as he could so that he could knock him down, but that would be extremely tough as this was an almost elephantine general. He tried to distract him. "Hey General, come here! "Nenthrate swiftly thrust his sword hard into Corsander's neck, making him fall down and leaving an opening for another attack. He swiped at his neck again, at the same spot. The General got up again and lunged forward trying to snatch the blade. Blados passed it towards Nenthrate. Corsander lunged forward to Nenthrate and he passed it to Blados. Blados gave it to Nenthrate again, and the General almost got it. Enough! As Corsander swiped at Nenthrate, a duplicate of Nenthrate appeared, Or was it just a hallucination from Nenthrate's exhaustion?

Blados hit Corsander and at that exact moment Nenthrate fell. The explosion was gigantic...

Nenthrate woke up with a start. There was fire all around him. Blados had just recovered too. They were amazed that they hadn't died, but were only knocked out for several hours. "Are you okay?" asked Blados. "Yeah," said Nenthrate.

A few hours later, at the hall in which the lower Medbay, Inventory Room, Security Base and Restroom 2 could be found:

Nenthrate, Blados and Radrason walked through the normally full hall. After the stealthy attack by Corsander, people had started to take precautions of not going through the halls alone, and some people who were scared enough had set up a few booby traps without any warning, so Nenthrate usually found himself tripping over bombs which would explode on contact and Nenthrate took a long time to get to the hospital after he tripped on some of those obstacles. Blados took his Sapparator out, hoping to take the advantage of using it after a long time to defeat any General that came in their way. All of a sudden, Nenthrate heard a creak in the hall one floor below. Could it be a general? They ran down in a panic. Nenthrate was not sure that there would be a General down there waiting for him. The God of Evil didn't usually send generals daily.

Thankfully, it was not a General but Sarparin. "Nenthrate?" He said in surprise. "I wanted to tell-" an annnouncement interrupted Sarparin. "Nenthrate to the 17th floor please." The voice sounded panicky. Nenthrate hurriedly made his way up. He discovered Techno engaged in a battle with a General. "Blados, now!" Nenthrate commanded. Blados swiftly sprang into action while Techno exited. He threw his blade at Nenthrate, who caught it skillfully. Blados moved backwards with surprising speed, sensing an opportunity, the General swung both arms backwards. Siezing the moment, when the General was vulnerable, Nenthrate transformed to deflect an incoming attack with one hand and threw the blade. Blados, on the other hand was busy handling the monster's counter attacks. As intended, the general turned back and Nenthrate hurled his sword on to his back. Blados ran forward to Nenthrate. This time, they would attack together. They both transformed into the same alien. The general was now confused as to who to swipe at.

Nenthrate went front but Blados stopped him. He knew the General only wanted Nenthrate dead. So he tricked him to give Nenthrate an advantage. Nenthrate understood. He hit him, and went back while Blados continued to fight. Suddenly, the General hit Blados. Hard. He was unconcious and Nenthrate ran forward with so much speed that the General couldn't hit him. Collecting every ounce of energy he had, he hit the General so hard that everything exploded in a fiery blast with Nenthrate in the centre of it.

Blados had regained consciousness shortly before this happened. "Nenthrate!!!" He screamed as he saw him being blasted into outer space, unconsious. He knew that he had lost him. Maybe for a long time. Maybe, forever. He told Techno and the others about this. He did this for us, said Blados. "We won't let him die just like that!"

"What just happened?!" said Nenthrate. He expected to see himself in the Medbay. Instead, he found himself on the rough ground of another planet. He rubbed his head. Ow! He said. He touched his face. He could feel blood dripping. He fell down again. He could feel immense pain in his forehead, jaw and leg. He couldn't get up. Finally, he fainted. Some time later, he found someone checking him. He tried to get up and fight him, but he couldn't. "Easy now," said the strange person. "I'm not gonna hurt you." "Who are you?" asked Nenthrate. "Gerados," he replied. "How did you find me?" "I found you in the dark forest. Not a good place to be in. I saw all the blood on your face and thought a wild creature had hurt you." "No, it wasn't a wild creature," replied Nenthrate. "I got separated from my family." He looked at Gerados pensively, as if trying to solve a riddle.

Just as Gerados was about to say something, Nenthrate asked, "What's your full name?" Gerados Solaris. Gerados haltingly told him that he reminded him of his brother. Nenthrate said, "I am indeed Nenthrate Solaris, and you are my cousin." A hug was badly needed but not possible because of Nenthrate's severe wounds, so they just shook hands softly but warmly. "Is Blados dead?" Gerados questioned. "No," said Nenthrate. He narrated to him all that had happened till now.

A month later, when the others found Nenthrate...

Nenthrate's medication is almost finished, said Gerados to Techno, Blados and Sarparin who were busy looking at Nenthrate worriedly. They were deeply grateful to Gerados for having found Nenthrate when he did and tending to his wounds so open – heartedly. Nenthrate slowly opened his eyes. He was smiling. Not in that pleasant way that shows you're happy, but in that cold, dark way that strikes fear into others' hearts... that shows you're evil. Nenthrate tried to hit Techno but Blados deflected the blow with his shield. Nenthrate pushed the shield aside with one hand and tried to hit them both with the other. Suddenly, he started to transform into a monster. Two extra arms tore out of his skin turning into knive hands. The other two became metal. His hair turned to ash and flew away in the dust, replaced by spikes. Shields emerged out of nowhere onto his arms. He could breathe fire through his mouth just like a dragon. His feet got bigger and redder, and he grew in size. His chest became metal and his legs had lava on them. His body became devoid of human skin. His teeth became sharp as knives, and a pair of wings sprouted onto his back. He was a truly terrifying sight! Blados was scared although he tried not to show it. Techno was too.

When he talked, it sounded like two Gods of Evil were in one room, confident of smashing everyone and everything within range.

"Who wants to fight now?" He breathed in deeply and exhaled. 50 smaller Monster- Nenthrates emerged by his sorcery. Blados ran forward. Monster-Nenthrate knocked him to the wall with his full force. A guard came in to fight. Monster- Nenthrate smashed him to the ground where he lay dead. "This is what will happen to you if you try to fight—OW!" Blados had hit Monster – Nenthrate with some of the strongest blades that ever existed. He could do this because he had transformed into Bladrix. But Nenthrate transformed into something beyond Blados' power: Ultimate Lavaran. Blados transformed into Ultracranos. Ultracranos looked tiny as compared to Ultimate Lavaran. Monster – Nenthrate smashed Blados to the ground where he lay either injured or dead. Nenthrate's father tried to stop him but he picked him up and threw him on Blados. The same happened with Techno and Sarparin. He left the Medbay and Gerados was the only one unharmed. "HAHAHA!" He laughed maniacally. "The fools."

A month later...

Blados woke up with a start. The others were slowly regaining consiousness. There was blood everywhere- on their body, face, legs, feet, back and more. "I can't understand why Nenthrate adopted that Monster Mode." Gerados said, " My hypothesis is that it's because everything has become unstable compared to the massive amount of power Nenthrate has." "Speaking of Nenthrate, why did he show us mercy? Maybe he thought you were already dead or experienced a flashback on how he was so close to you." Techno said, "I can find a way to communicate with Nenthrate."

"What is it?" asked Monster – Nenthrate rudely when she tried to get through. "Nenthrate, please"— "Oh please," interrupted Monster – Nenthrate. "Not the peace talk now But I do have something to say to all of you. Come next month at midnight, to the beach and I will give you the fiercest fight of your life. Surely you will need to practice till then. If you run scared and don't come, I will track you down and kill each one of you. Train hard and fight well... "And choose your words well. They might just be your last. Good luck! You'll need it."

The others suffered multiple rough nights. They started training nervously- trying out new moves, new angles, and new strikes. Soon they were pushing their bodies to the limit and sweating from it all. They had realised that fighting as one entity together was their only hope. They knew that deep inside the Monster Nenthrate, their old buddy Nenthrate was still trapped in there, trying to help in some way. Blados said, "we won't kill Nenthrate or Monster – Nenthrate." "We'll wound him badly so that he won't be able to hurt any of us anymore. Then, Gerados can try and turn him back to normal. Got it?" he asked. "Just one thing," piped up Gerados. "How will we be able to defeat Monster - Nenthrate? I mean, he's strong. Or stronger than before. We might be able to defeat him perhaps, but what about his aliens? That'll be a toughie." Blados thought for a second, then he said, "We'll make him transform into every alien and then analyze his attacks, and then we'll be able to bring him down." Gerados thought for a moment, and said, "Hey, that's not such a bad idea!" "But we'll have to hold him off for that much longer." Blados said. So they practised more and soon, the month was over, and the day they had feared had come. They had to fight Nenthrate.

"So, you've come," said Monster - Nenthrate with a grin. "It'll be fun to finish you off. "We're not giving up on you," said Techno. "Are you sure?" Asked Monster - Nenthrate with a raised eyebrow. Blados sighed and replied... "Yes." Then, said Monster - Nenthrate with an evil sneer. "Hiyaaaaaa!!!!!" His battle cry sounded terrifying. There was fire rising behind him. I don't need 2 hands to defeat you! To prove it, he let Techno, Blados and Sarparin rush upon him together. He put his hand down for them to climb on. He shook them off the moment they touched him. "Attack together!!!" screamed Blados as he rushed in for another attack. Nenthrate hit Blados but there was one thing he didn't realise. Sarparin was on him and as soon as Sarparin realised he had an opportunity, he hit him hard on the neck. "Hey," said Nenthrate to Sarparin. "Not COOL!" He hit him and he fell and was immediately immobolised. Monster - Nenthrate looked back toward Blados. Gerados silently picked up Sarparin and took him to the Medbay. Blados was steaming now. "RAAAAAAH!!!" He roared like a fierce lion pouncing on his prey. Monster - Nenthrate simply laughed like... well I don't know! He hit Blados with full force. Luckily, Blados escaped with a mere surface wound. A sword in his left leg made him limp.

"Nenthrate, stop now!!!" He screamed. Nenthrate smiled, and was about to punch him when he stopped. He held his head and screamed loudly- a cry so piercing it could have exploded one's eardrums – "AAAAAAARRRRRRGGH!!!!!!!!" He suddenly transformed back into the normal Nenthrate, with scars and bruises everywhere. One of his wounds in his stomach was deep. His clothes were torn and he was unconscious but Blados thought that he might still be alive. I mean, all those times we thought that he was dead but he survived.

A year later:

It had taken a long time for Nenthrate to get better. The wounds were worse than they looked and the seasons led to complications, slowing down the amount of time the wounds needed to heal completely. Nenthrate got up at 4:39 in the afternoon after a long time. He looked different and his 27th birthday had passed. He got up and saw he was alone. *Why would the others abandon me?* He thought. At that moment, he had no memory of what he'd done, but suddenly he remembered it all. A quick flashback showed him laughing evilly, killing a guard, transforming and almost killing Blados. After that, he found the others right outside. They all took out their weapons and stunned him. "It's me guys." Nenthrate said right after they stopped trying to kill him. "Yo, sorry for it all. I was in chains inside the evil that had posessed me. I did what he commanded. I finally broke free and hit him hard. I'm sorry. That's all I can say. I was out of control."

Meanwhile...

The God of Evil's ship started to close in silently onto Nenthrate's. "Ready the blasters," he said with a smile.

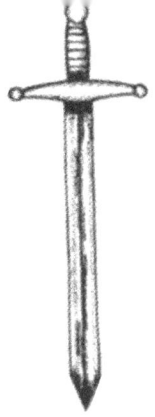

The war begins

BREEEP! BREEEEEEP!!! The alarm sounded. Something was coming at them with terrifying force. Missiles were coming towards the ship with fire raging behind them. The sound of chaos filled the air. A woman with a black jacket streaked past the control centre. Techno was trying to dodge some of the missiles but she knew that the ship would be an easy target since it was so big. After 40 minutes, the missiles were still coming towards them. Nenthrate took control. He turned the ship around and went right next to The God of Evil's ship as the missiles streaked after him. He moved just a moment before it became too late to save the ship from the powerful missiles. He shot a missile to counter it and for some reason, The God of Evil's missile wasn't too dense so it rebounded and hit The God of Evil's ship instead. Nenthrate took a deep breath and said, "LET'S GET OUT OF HERE!!!" in a panicky voice. There was still chaos everywhere. Nenthrate unsuccessfully tried to calm down a few people who were floundering.

A few weeks after New year, 28th January, to be precise:

Nenthrate ran to a safe spot, right behind a blackish wall. He saw The God of Evil go past him. He wouldn't dare make a sound. He felt his heart pounding in his chest. Techno and Blados were 7 feet away from him, on a different wall. They were in some sort of maze. The God of Evil hit a random wall hard. It smashed to pieces. Thankfully, nobody was there. Nenthrate knew that The God of Evil would find him somehow, and so he gave Techno and Blados the attack together signal. They all fired at The God of Evil.

Two shots hit, and one missed. Techno's arrow hit a trap instead. They quickly shifted columns. The problem was, that The God of Evil flew in the air, high above the maze and saw the trio running. Techno and Blados were at the same spot but Nenthrate was alone. The God of Evil fired a blast

The war begins

which could have been fatal. Nenthrate noticed this in time and swiftly moved aside. Fire was behind him and a trap in front of him. He was stuck between the devil and the deep sea. He jumped onto the trap and "*spriiiiiing!!!*" He flew for a second, but then started falling to the ground. BOOOM!!! The sound of this crash was deafening. Before he "died" he heard the others scream: Nenthrate!!!

Nenthrate woke up with a start. "That was one terrifying dream. Man, I gotta learn how Gerados sleeps without dreams like this." A Y 7 9 Z S D Y, he said, to open the door. Techno! Blados! He screamed. Nobody came. OK, he said, let me search for them. He walked into Techno's room. Empty. The same with Blados' room. In the hall, he saw Blados armed and Monster – Nenthrate. Not this again. He grunted. They turned and ran toward him. Techno stood behind. She walked forward menacingly, to finish him off. AAAAARGH!!! He screamed.

WHOA! Nenthrate said as he woke up. A dream in a dream. That's weird, he said. He heard a distant bang. Krakaboom!!! A general, I suspect, he said with a tone of suspicion. Is this another dream? It looked very real. Nenthrate found Blados, Techno and Sarparin battling with five generals. What the— Nenthrate said in surprise. He joined the battle. The others were pushed back. Nenthrate fought wildly. He managed to inflict some damage on a general, but they were working together. Nenthrate transformed into a new alien from his Sapparator.

He named it Heatlite because when any of the generals touched it, the part which dared to touch Nenthrate would burn to a crisp because of his white hot rage. Still, he couldn't destroy the generals, only managing to disable them for a while.

By this time, Blados had planned a surprise attack. While the generals were busy fighting Nenthrate, he inflicted some damage and Techno did the same thing. Blados inflicted a surface wound which was barely visible as Nenthrate was moving fast, blocking the view of the general. Nenthrate tried to confuse them and land a blow or two at the same time. He ran between two pairs of arms on each side directed at him and managed to hit two of the generals on his right without getting hit back. "I don't need my aliens to finish them." He managed to hit out again, but this time, he was not so lucky. The other generals hit him together. He couldn't stand it. They hit him hard on the face. He was bleeding. Blood and adrenaline were rushing through his veins. His Sapparator got affected too and exploded. It was hard to fight now. His vision was beginning to blur. The others jumped

The war begins

forward. Warm darkness was starting to envelop him. The others fought with all their strength while Nenthrate tried to survive the heavy blows.

A week later, when Nenthrate had regained consciousness:

"Whoa…" he said as he waved his hand in front of his face. "That was crazy." He sighed. The blood had dried up on his face, but the scars remained. Nenthrate looked at the room. It was empty. He didn't notice that in the window, The God of Evil's ship was visible.

Bang! Bang!! Bang!!!

The reverbrating noise on the ship alarmed many, as they thought it was a general but no, it was not. An entire army of millions of monsters stood at the entrance to the ship. WHAAA- *The God of Evil wasn't joking when he had said he possesed a huge army- I can't handle all of this alone*, thought Nenthrate. What is that?! said Blados. Techno arrived on the scene. So did Sarparin and Gerados. The humans on the ship were mobilizing but inside their hearts was their hidden weakness: fear… Though the numbers were equal, the strength remained imbalanced. The God of Evil laughed. He had found them. He walked forward and started pacing around the massive amount of people that had gathered as if he was inspecting them.

When he saw Nenthrate, he smiled. "What's that for?" said Nenthrate ferociously. Nenthrate ran toward The God of Evil, trying to hit him. The God of Evil stood there, waiting for him to come. Nenthrate missed and accidentally hit the magnet button. Nenthrate watched as planets clumped together and a giant explosion wiped out all life on these planets. The entire area transformed into a battlefield- quite a big one indeed. Nenthrate hit again and, this time, the sword went through a few generals.. He understood that this was not the real deal, but only a projection of his army.

The giant planet looked dangerous. Why would The God of Evil send a projection? Nenthrate asked himself. Meanwhile, on his ship, The God of Evil put his hand in the air, as if trying to hit some invisible foe. "The plan worked perfectly, my Lord." exclaimed Veldos. "I know that, you bonehead," said The God of Evil calmly. "Do not spoil my joy," he said mischievously. "The time has come to neutralise the threat.

To exterminate The Enemy- Nenthrate." He said this with a mix of piercing ferocity and slight happiness. "Come on. To the edge of the Seleste Universe!"

"What's that?" asked Nenthrate. "The book? That's Hyponsor Asretor Solglopno Nocrinos (The Battle of Infinity's 500 most epic moves Non-Abridged)" said Blados. "Hypo what?" said Nenthrate. "Doesn't matter," replied Blados. "It's a strange book, really, all in Yonosricoran," Said. Blados "Yono what?" asked Techno. "Yonosricoran. Before you found me, I lived with the Yonosricorans. They were scared of a beast your size, Nenthrate. I destroyed the beast. But I missed the head, it was like a pumpkin. As a gift, they gave me this." He held the book up. Nenthrate saw a mark on it. A mark that looked familiar. It had a hand on it, tiny traces of blood which looked like they were trickling down the hand, and a body beside it. It was surprisingly tiny. Blados rambled on—"those aliens were so tiny and harmless. You should have seen them. They could have made you think you were hallucinating. So cute! I tell you. If I ever see one again, I'm going to use him as a pillow." Techno was listening with full interest. Nenthrate meanwhile, was not paying attention to Blados' rambling. He was more interested in the strange mark. He had remembered when he had last seen it: as a child. Although he couldn't remember who's mark it was, he knew he had seen it before. He thought that this was some sort of clue, but he could not fully recognise it yet.

This is a major problem. Nenthrate thought. *I wonder if this is the divine key to discovering all the true secrets of The God of Evil. AARRGHH! What's the use? It'll probably lead me to some dead end. It's like a maze, this war. I don't think I'll ever get out of it alive. I mean—* Nenthrate's thoughts were interrupted by Blados and Techno. "Nenthrate!!!" they yelled. "What's the matter?" "This book." Nenthrate replied, still engrossed with the mark. They came closer and saw the mark. "What is this?" asked Blados. Techno tried to reassure them. "We'll worry about that later.

We have more to do." Honestly, I don't think any of them felt reassured. They all walked into their separate rooms, with a ghostly feeling in their stomachs.

"Bam! Bam!" Nenthrate and Sarparin were engaged in a practice duel, in an area which had many hiding places. They often told each other where they had gone wrong. Nenthrate hid in the tree, just above Sarparin and Sarparin got confused. "Come out, come out wherever you are!" said Sarparin. That sentence was repeated time and again. Nenthrate jumped down and Sarparin said, "Wrong move." He moved his sword forward, and almost hit Nenthrate before he stopped. "No," said Nenthrate. "You made the wrong move. I could have easily bent down and thrown my blade at you. And even if I was not quick enough to do that, my shield would have blocked it. Then your knives would get stuck, I would take it out and then I would have the advantage." "Oh," said Sarparin. "Nice. Should have thought of that." "Hey Nenthrate," a voice said. He turned. He saw the unusually downcast face of Radrason. "What's the matter?" said Nenthrate feeling that something was wrong. "The matter is, the ship is falling. Someone hit the engine. A general or a- whatever. The point is, I would appreciate it if you would help me in fixing the engines. I'm not good at fixing stuff." "Ask Techno." Nenthrate replied breezily. "OK," said Radrason and he left the room, accidentally banging the doors behind him.

"Why is he so sad? He knows Techno'll fix it in a jiffy." "Exactly," said Sarparin. "Man, that's crazy."

But Sarparin didn't notice a general sneaking up behind Nenthrate. Nenthrate did though. He pretended to look distracted. Then, when the general was close enough, he hit him with his sword.

Sarparin saw this and inched forward while the general was fighting Nenthrate and hit him with his sword. The general stepped back, to give himself a break. Then, he hid. Sarparin yelled: "COME OUT AND FIGHT, YOU STUPID—" he was interrupted by the general. "What did you call me?" the general said angrily. "Hiiyaaaaa!" He roared as he came out of a tree right next to the one Nenthrate hid in but little did he know that this was a ruse. He was about to hit Sarparin when Nenthrate took the blow on his shield. The general was hit by someone else: Blados. Techno was there too. "All right!" said Nenthrate with glee. The general was no match for all of them together. They kept hitting him and finally, he exploded in a fiery blast.

At 3:00 in the morning:

Nenthrate stood on Techno's ship. This was it. He knew he was close to 'it'. 'It's' destruction was coming nearer and nearer. Finally, all this would be over. Nenthrate knew that he might have to sacrifice himself in time, but he knew it would be for a good cause. He knew that if he died, his friends would avenge him. But one thing that worried him the most was his friends themselves. What if they failed to continue the unfinished tasks he left behind? The entire Multiverse was at stake. After all, "it" was one of the most powerful fighters of all time. But then it struck him. He was equally powerful. The one whose destiny was to vanquish "it". Even if it meant dying in the ultimate battle. The pieces of the puzzle were coming together. The more he thought about this eternal yet nauseating topic, the more he understood it.

"*Give it a rest, Nenthrate!*" *he said. He sighed and allowed the smooth feeling of space to creep upon him.*

Three seconds later in his bedroom, "WHOA!"exclaimed Nenthrate. His eyes were slowly recognising where he was. He was... on the floor? Must've been a bad dream, Nenthrate thought. He picked himself up from the clean floor. He looked at his bedside table, hoping to find a note. Sure enough, there was one. He read it:

Dear Nenthrate

If you are reading this note, then you must read it to the last word. If it's not 10:00, then you should go back to sleep. You have a lot to do. And before you sleep, brush. OK?

Sincerely

Techno

Nenthrate smiled and brushed for about 2 minutes following Techno's advice, and then went back to sleep, and even in this tough time, he looked happy...

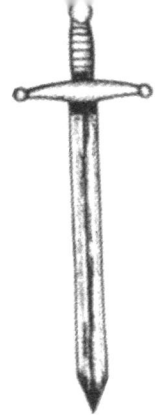

True Path

At 10:00, Nenthrate switched off his alarm. He got up, looked at his messages on the phone and... "What in the"--- 189 messages were marked unread. "I want the samples of the document you promised me! Autographs? The mail guy is showering messages. Tell him to send it to the supreme commander!" He had forgotten about yesterday. He had to sign 236 contracts. In short, let's just say he had a busy day. He wrote the document to Ceron, the human whom he had promised. He had only 3 hours to finish all the work. The next 2 hours melted away like butter. He had to send a dozen instructions to the mailroom guy on how to sort out the mails and distribute them to different parts of the ship. This altogether took 2 hours. Then he had to send his autographs to the Candy Planet (Chapter 3) They had heard about his heroic acts and made him their idol. Well, he certainly is a hero so he deserves that respect. He was finishing a call with the security telling them the new defence plans when another call came. Luckily, he had finished telling them how to carry out the orders. Nenthrate cut the call, reached toward the other phone and answered it. It was Techno. "What's the matter?" Techno said, "God of Evil." Techno said. "Probably just a projection," replied Nenthrate with an exhausted sigh. On Techno's end, she acknowledged and scanned space for the projector. "Nope, it's real," said Techno worriedly. "Very real…"

"OK then," said Nenthrate. "I'm ready. " This is what he'd been preparing for. This is how it started. Nenthrate geared up. He got an RPG. He wore armour with the Solaris logo on it. He put on his helmet with a click. He looked forward with determination. Meanwhile, everybody was in the Cockpit, watching the intense battle. Two missiles were fired from Techno's ship and The God of Evil reacted to this assault quickly. He shot another two missiles and they both exploded in mid-air because they had touched each other. He did this exactly when Nenthrate shot his missiles. They both understood. It was a matter of who shot first. Whoever was distracted would be dead. General Receran jumped forward as he saw what The God of Evil had missed. Two smaller missiles were coming at them with terrifying speed and force. The first missile missed but the second one hit them. "YES!" said Nenthrate, punching the air. "NO!" screamed The God of Evil. All of a sudden, Nenthrate turned left.

Then right.

Left again.

Right again.

He kept doing this and Techno started to feel dizzy. "What are you doing?" she said, turning green. "I am creating confusion so that The God of Evil's missiles don't get a clear shot. Nenthrate said plainly.

"The perfect time for a strategic attack like this…" said Techno. "Good observation", muttered Nenthrate, not focused on Techno right now. He was getting a strange feeling that The God of Evil was planning something much bigger. Just then, Snitchel went into his trance again. Oh, that's just great, said Blados sarcastically.

"I'll deal with him, you stay here." "I'll come too," said Radrason. Blados took a hit from Snitchel's swords on his shields. Meanwhile, Radrason, seeing the advantage leapt to be able to hit Snitchel whenever possible. Blados said: " You're a fair fighter." Nenthrate was focusing on The God of Evil. He saw him in the distance. Suddenly, an idea struck him. I'm going aboard, said Nenthrate. "You mean we're." Blados had got rid of Snitchel and walked toward Nenthrate. "No." said Nenthrate. "You'll get hurt." "But—" Nenthrate ignored Blados, turned and walked out to the *Exit* door which made Blados pause mid-sentence. Nenthrate suddenly turned and came back. "You're right," he said. "We're in this together." Blados had difficulty not smiling. "Nothing's wrong with smiling openly," said Nenthrate. "Right," grinned Blados. Nenthrate flew the ship out of The God of Evil's line of sight. "War's on!!!" he roared.

The God of Evil's ship, at 5:00 PM:

"My Lord, "said a General worriedly. "Are you OK?" "I'm fine!" said The God of Evil with annoyance in his voice. "The insolent fool, Nenthrate got away! And I won't die so easily. We can't keep losing like this. Any General who fails me in battle and survives Nenthrate's wrath, not that it's more than mine, will die. I would have easily dodged the blast if you hadn't pushed me aside." The General recoiled. The God of Evil's anger was legendary. The

God of Evil lunged forward and ripped off the general's head. He fell and exploded. By this time, all of the Generals had awoken and were forced to witness this awful sight. Some of them squirmed visibly. How horrible could he- (The God of Evil) be? "There is only one General, The God of Evil announced, that I can rely on; Eronostal."

Eronostal stepped forward and bowed to The God of Evil. "It is an honour to serve you." "Understand all this?" he asked everybody. They all nodded at the same time. Clearly, they understood.

Nenthrate stood on a platform designed to look out the window. He still couldn't understand the meaning of that symbol on the cover page of Hyponsor Asretor Solglopno Nocrinos- Blados' book. "I hope that he- The God of Evil doesn't find us." he said, sensing Techno was behind him. She put her hand on his shoulder. Nenthrate didn't look back. Suddenly, he fell. Techno looked back and saw a General. *Dammit*, she thought as she turned around fully to face the fresh danger.

Nenthrate got up. Techno said, "Thank God you're OK." He had barely missed a blow from the General. *Not bad*, he thought. He faced the General and thought he was hallucinating. Techno saw it too. "No way..." Nenthrate said to Techno. It was The

God of Evil. "Oh yeah!" smirked The God of Evil. "Who's the star of the show now?" he said. "Since when do you say that?" questioned Nenthrate. "None of your business," he said rudely as he knocked him off his feet while putting his other hand around Techno. Then he picked up an unconscious Nenthrate and threw him and Techno down. Techno touched the ground a few miliseconds before Nenthrate. Nenthrate was slowly regaining consciousness but the general pushed him down again. He was hurt. Techno watched helplessly as Nenthrate bled furiously. Techno was bleeding much less than Nenthrate as The God of Evil had let her live. She took a bit of Nenthrate's cape and put it around his chest to staunch the bleeding. She knew it was only a matter of time before the others arrived. She had to keep Nenthrate alive till then. She got up and hit The God of Evil. She missed and destroyed the general instead.

He had been expecting this. He simply pushed her onto Nenthrate's wound. The part of the cape that staunched the blood flow came off quickly. Techno was despairing. Luckily, Sarparin and Blados came to their rescue. Blados moved forward menacingly towards The God of Evil while Sarparin came to take Nenthrate to the Medbay. Blados' next blow just scraped by The God of Evil. "Ughhh! Gotta think of a way to bring him down." Blados saw a bright blue button on his chest just before The God of Evil fled. "Hmm," he said.

Nenthrate's wounds had swelled to an enormous size. He was still unconscious because a few of his injuries could not possibly heal in fewer than 2- 3 months. "I don't think that The God of Evil came just to scare us. I think he wanted something more. How did he suddenly grow stronger?!" Blados said. Techno wasn't listening. She was busy looking at Nenthrate. "I wonder if this has something to do with the mark on Hyponsor Asretor Solglopno Nocrinos." "I think you're on the right track," said Gerados looking at Blados.

A month later: (June 27th)

First of all, don't worry, Nenthrate's better. Oh well, let me continue with the story. Nenthrate looked in the mirror. "Augh!!!" He screamed when he saw the wound on his face. It made him look really... different. Blados couldn't stop laughing. Nenthrate didn't find it funny though. And he had very good reasons why. But let's not talk about that. "Was the fight that hard?!" he said. "It must have been bad. How did The God of Evil ever get this strong?" "I dunno," said Blados. "Big problem. The last time you saw him he was getting his butt kicked. This time it was the complete opposite! It was like he was someone else. But dammit!" he said in frustration. "Of course!" "What?" asked Techno, confused.

"He must've not been The God of Evil at all! Must be a strong general who could shapeshift!" said Blados. "That connects with the blue button I saw on him. If we can press that button without him shapeshifting..." We need to make a plan before he comes back again. " I'm on it," said Nenthrate.

As soon they had settled in their rooms an alarm rang. Techno picked up her walkie talkie and exclaimed excitedly "Talk of the devil- the general is back as I suspected. This is our chance." They met in the hall and made their plan: Techno would sneak up and play the part of the distraction. Then Blados would execute the real plan- it was to get him slowly but surely to a rope that was sturdy enough to switch off the button. In case the general noticed the rope, as the final measure, Nenthrate would battle the monster one to one. (he insisted on that part). "This time" growled the general / The God of Evil "Nenthrate won't survive." "Get ready," whispered Nenthrate. Techno nodded and jumped into action. She went through the hallway behind the general while the others stood in wait. When they heard a sound- BAM, then Nenthrate took his place and so did Blados. Blados went left and Nenthrate went right, silently. Techno was duelling furiously with the monster; both were fighting to kill. She kept aiming for the monster's chest, trying to switch off the button. Blados gave a thumbs–up. Techno tried to give one back but she got hit by his massive sword. She grunted in pain as she got knocked off her feet. Nenthrate nodded. Blados knew this meant- " it's only us now. " Nenthrate could hear the clang of swords and the battle cries every two seconds...

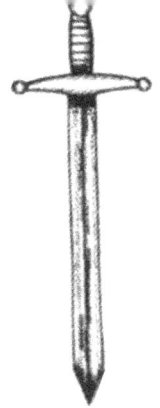

Time to fight

Night fell. Nenthrate saw someone's shadow. He couldn't make out if it was Blados or the general. The hallway in which the fight had taken place was silent. Nenthrate was alert, for he didn't know what the next move would be and who would strike. He stood there, sword at the ready. He was breathing silently, waiting for an attack. He heard a noise and he stepped back. The noise echoed through the large and dark corridor. He hesitated for a moment, then crept forward and onto the side of the wall, feeling around for anything unusual and then grasped something- a big, circular object. He wanted to run but something... something was rooting him to the spot. For a second, he thought that he was done for, but at the same instant he realised it was only a decoration on one of the pillars holding up the ceiling. Then he felt the eerie silence around him. He shivered at the thought that fear could render him powerless, even though momentarily. He waited and watched till morning. He suddenly saw what had happened. The General was lying dead while Blados was pinned to the wall. A sword had almost ripped off a part of Blados' neck and he looked quite limp. On closer examination it turned out that it was not a mortal wound. He was sent to the hospital immediately but the ship had run out of fuel and was about to crash on a strange planet. "CRAKABOOM!" The ship exploded on a red land: Entaros! Their original homeland! It was looking untouched as there appeared to be no sign of life anywhere. Just then, another ship crashed onto Entaros not far from them. It was massive. A cloud of dust blinded them.

When they could see again, The God of Evil stood in front of them. "Nenthrate," he said in his high, cold and clear voice. "Long time no see. I guess it's time for the ultimate war. As you can see, I've been gathering a few old comrades." Nenthrate gasped. There was Lorcrandos, Fendilin and more. But then

Time to fight

he remembered that he had an army too. "We're not afraid of you!" He shouted in his bravest voice. "Oh really?" The God of Evil asked. Nenthrate didn't feel good. Then he thought of all his friends and felt braver. He ran forward. The others did too. *It's now or never*, he thought. "Hiyaaa!" Suddenly, everybody, except a few people, stepped back. 3 duels were happening simultaneously: Gerados and Glomon were duelling furiously, swords clanging, Blados and Ferinar, and Techno and Metagorn.

Nenthrate saw a really big and muscular General try to enter one battle but Nenthrate stopped him just as The God of Evil came in and hit him hard. He went down. The God of Evil tried to kill him with a blast but a few humans came in front of him and died instead. He fell backwards. The God of Evil activated a trap: Spikes covered 5 – 6 square feet. Due to the way he fell, Nenthrate was lying on his back. Blados rushed toward him and made a spectacular move: he kicked The God of Evil and the general viciously, knocking them down and teleported with Nenthrate instantly (it was a new invention Techno was working on) to the Medbay while the fight continued. Someone else emerged. Techno tried to remove the black hood that shadowed his face. He simply kicked her aside and walked forward. The crowd moved aside for this black figure. He went toward the Medbay. The God of Evil tried to stop him but he got kicked so hard that he went flying backwards into his own army...

The God of Evil mumbled something, inaudible to any of the onlookers. After that strange person was out of sight, the tomblike silence was interrupted by the resuming sounds of the war, as there was no further reason to pause. Nenthrate at the moment was not conscious and was trapped in his own mind. In the flashback in his subconcious mind, moments of his life were racing before his eyes rapidly. Nenthrate was stunned by this magical sight. At one time he thought he felt someone touching him but it was just the wind. Am I dead? He thought. The answer came to him, clear and strong: "No, I can't die. I refuse to do so. My life has not gone full circle, my mission in life is not complete." Before his untimely death, his grandfather had told him " You are not ordinary. Things are going to happen in your life. They will be... beyond anyone's imagination..." Enough with that!

He was going to get out of this place. He looked around and as far as the eye could see, there was white, white, white. He walked around, ran in one direction, hoping to see something, anything. Argh!

He punched the ground several times. He accidentally punched himself. Ouch! But... could he be dead? His eyes opened. He looked at himself. He didn't look the same. He looked 10- 15 inches taller. His eyes were now totally black, not brown. His mouth was slightly shorter. His arms were longer and on his head, he felt like a car had hit him. He wriggled his hand a little. *Great. At least I know I'm not immobolised,* Nenthrate thought. The next two things he thought were, "Where can I be?" The answer automatically came to him: *in the Medbay. Everyone must have been worried about me.* He tried to speak. He was able to speak, but he must have aquired a new voice because it was deeper.

He stood up and walked across the Medbay. Its look had changed. He bumped into a strange figure. The same strange figure that pushed The God of Evil back. Nenthrate stepped back. The figure didn't say anything. He just walked a step forward. Nenthrate raised his eyebrow. "Hello?" He said. "I am The God of Evil's brother."

"What in the –" Nenthrate said, with disbelief. He looked for something to fight with but his thoughts were interrupted by The God of Evil's brother. "Whoa, I wouldn't do anything like that, he said quickly. My name is Arsicon, he said. I know that my brother is the Epitome of Evil and deserves to be destroyed, but I can't defeat him alone. "Tell me more" said Nenthrate, his curiosity piqued. I might be able to hold him off for a while but- oh I almost forgot. That General Crashpilot betrayed you." "I'm not surprised," said Nenthrate, rolling his eyes. As you might remember, he never trusted Crashpilot. "Plus, any information about The God of Evil he gave you was fake. So that's why we haven't defeated him yet," said Nenthrate thoughtfully. Arsicon's next words stunned Nenthrate. "The Ultimate Soul is the source of his power," whispered Arsicon. "The Ultimate *what?!*" Said Nenthrate jumping up. "I thought that was destroyed a thousand years ago? What- "Arsicon answered all his questions with one answer; The God of Evil faked the illusion, and confided his deepest darkest secret, only in me." Nenthrate remembered how he had questioned Snitchel. *"He shared his deepest, darkest secret." "Tell me! Is it the key to destroying him?"* Snitchel had then taken out those swords from nowhere. Suddenly, it all clicked into place. "The God of Evil wanted to rule the Multiverse as a power – hungry tyrant, without anyone being in his way, *of course!* He thought that the key to his immortality was hidden forever...

But, he confided in you and that was the undoing of his plans." "Well, he wouldn't think of his own brother betraying him, right?" Arsicon said. "That's crazy! If you would have not come here and told me, I would have never been able to destroy him," Nenthrate said. "It makes perfect sense!" Now, he just had to track down the Ultimate Soul.

He looked at Arsicon, expecting him to tell him the location of the Ultimate Soul, and then it would all be over but... "I don't know. He would never tell me that part of the secret," he said sadly. "I think he suspected something like this" "No!!!" cried Nenthrate. His hope for an early end to this battle between Good and Evil was at an all – time low. "Wait!" Arsicon said. "Don't lose heart! The information I am going to give you now will certainly lead you to victory even though you will have to strive and struggle still more." "The God of Evil divided The Ultimate Soul into four fragments" "He hid each of them well and if you find one, the next will be even harder to find... that's for sure." "Thanks, Nenthrate said. The war is happening below. We have to try and stop it first." "Oh sure! That's just great! Thank you sooo much, God of Evil!" Nenthrate said sarcastically He got up, and tried to walk off but was stopped by Arsicon. You are not gonna just stroll down there and say, " Hey there, I'm Nenthrate! I'm just gonna go now and find the Ultimate Soul! You're gonna die! You gotta plan this perfectly." "Oh yeah..." Nenthrate said. "I forgot." "Oh, lucky you have me," said Arsicon. "Don't boast," Nenthrate laughed. He liked Arsicon's friendly sense of humor and his seriousness. He was perfectly balanced, ready for war and kind, all qualities that Nenthrate valued. "So now... what shall we do," Arsicon said. "Sneak out," Nenthrate and Arsicon said in unison.

Nenthrate moved like an extremely stealthy ninja, navigating the halls of the ship. It was once fully functional but now it was broken and it felt unusual and eerie, like someone or something was watching him. More than once, he had to hide from the generals.It seemed they had won the battle below, and had taken everyone prisoner. *Blados, Techno, Gerados, Sarparin,* Nenthrate thought. What happened to them? He had no time to figure that out. He didn't want to abandon his friends, but he had no choice. This was bigger than that and would help all of them in the end. *If there was an end...* Nenthrate thought.

He walked forward. Finally, he made his way out of the twisting and turning halls using the last resort exit. He saw blood everywhere, but even that was not enough to make him turn back. He was no longer afraid. Now that he was in the open, he loaded a weapon just in case someone had dared to follow him. Hmm... he said quietly. He turned around quickly. Nobody was there. He narrowed his eyes, as if expecting someone to think that he had spotted him or her, or at least see him go out into the dark. Nobody. But he didn't notice a stranger looking at him patiently. This stranger didn't attack, but it definitely seemed on his mind? What stopped the stranger? Was it a feeling that now was not the right time? Who exactly was he?

Nenthrate walked on, not exactly knowing where he was. *If the God of Evil has attacked me on this planet, it could have been out of fear. Perhaps he thought I knew about the existence of the Ultimate Soul. I did not know earlier, but now I do,* Nenthrate thought. Suddenly, another more important thought struck him.

Where could the Ultimate Soul be? If I don't know and don't have the tiniest bit of information, what should I do? This will be an impossible task. He looked around, as if he was missing something.

Sure enough, he *was* missing something! A pair of footprints were on the rocky surface of the planet. After a thorough search for any leads, he chanced upon those footprints. Honestly, until this moment, he hadn't paid much attention to his surroundings and hadn't seen the strange man either. He followed the footprints like a detective, and finally came to a clearing where the footprints ended. *Of course this would happen,* he thought. "I better start searching" he said aloud without thinking.

At once, he realised he had made a wrong move, so he quickly took cover behind some rocks up ahead. After a while, he heard soft voices and realised someone was approaching. "Found you," a voice whispered. Nenthrate looked behind and saw The God of Evil coming for him. He decided it was best that he pretended that he had not seen him and spring a surprise attack. Little did he know that it was too late for that. He walked out, pretending as if nothing had happened.

More than once, his instincts told him to run, but he pretended he was navigating the ship, which made him feel a lot calmer than usual. He walked a little faster when he saw The God of Evil come closer, but that turned out to be his one big mistake. The God of Evil saw this and said, " This plan worked for a while, but not anymore!" He broke into a run. So did Nenthrate. "How did you come here?!" Nenthrate asked while running. "I followed you," said The God of Evil. "Your friends have escaped me again and the humans put up a good fight. Only five of my generals remain.

"They're dead?" Nenthrate said. "What else, you fool?" The God of Evil raged. Nenthrate ran faster. "Oh, and I sent a monster to destroy- what is their place called? Oh, Atlantis." "Why do you want to wreak this much havoc? "Nenthrate said. "Because that's what I was born to do..." The God of Evil said. Nenthrate's rage erupted like a volcano, he attacked The God of Evil with all he had. They both fell to the ground locked in fierce struggle.

They got up, and saw the bodies of two humans. Nenthrate calmed down a little and resumed the search. "Maybe I had missed something about those footprints- they had reappeared, but how?" Nenthrate thought aloud. "What footprints?" The God of Evil said. Apparently, he had not noticed the footprints so far, which was a relief for Nenthrate. What did he mean by *escaped?* Had Blados and the others been locked up prisoners? Luckily, while he was thinking, The God of Evil also looked confused and tired. Nenthrate took this as an opportunity to give him the slip.

The God of Evil searched around briefly when he found Nenthrate gone but gave up soon enough and retraced his steps. Their short battle had seemed to take its toll on The God of Evil. Nenthrate ran back to the footprints hoping that they would provide a valuable clue this time- He assumed that perhaps something had changed in his absence.

It had! There was a crumpled piece of paper lying on the ground. He opened it. It said nothing. He turned it around, and it said *Go right to the end, then go back all the way to see if you have missed something*. He went to the last step, then went all the way back to where the footprints started, with the paper in his pocket. Nothing happened. He waited. Again, nothing. Why not? He looked at the paper. "*Go back all the way to see if you have missed something*" maybe something had changed on the paper. New words formed like a spell had been cast upon it. It said "One foot forward, one foot back."

He put one foot forward on the second set of footprints and a strange passageway opened. Nenthrate went in out of curiosity. You know the saying, "curiosity killed the cat?" Well, not this time. Nenthrate walked down the shadowy passageway. More than once, he thought he had reached the end but it seemed to go on and on. The good news finally came; he reached the end of the labyrinth.

Time to fight

The bad news was that he couldn't see a thing. He felt around for some wood. Thankfully, there was some. Rocks were no problem; they were all around him. He created fire to guide him and moved on. When he could see, he was *still* not at the end of the passage; it just made a right turn. He walked through a load of spiderwebs, encountered strange snakes that packed a punch but fought them off and went on deeper. He finally found an object that emitted a blinding light! What could that possibly be? Could it be what he was desperately searching for? Was it – could it be one of the four pieces of the Ultimate Soul? For what else could shine so dazzlingly, as if associated with an otherworldly power. Its aura was overwhelming. Nenthrate stood transfixed for what seemed like ages.

Soon, he regained a sense of the present and remarked " Well, that was quite a struggle, but in the end, it was well worth it surprisingly easy to find! ". He remembered what Arsicon had said. *"He hid each of them well and if you find one, the next will be even harder to find."* I will never find the other three parts! And even if I do that, The God of Evil will have won by then! It's hopeless, He complained.

He walked back to the surface, careful not to trigger any of the many traps that awaited him on the return journey. Yes, there was another passageway leading back, illuminated with the light from the burning torches that lined the stone walls of the passage. He finally found the surface. The sun was setting by now and it was getting dark. Initially he decided to sleep for the night, but changed his mind. While resting, he thought he heard a noise, as if the ship which had crashed was flying high above him, but that was probably just a dream. Strangely, tonight he did not dream. He usually dreamt, but since the war, that had taken away from him everyone and everything he loved, his mind seemed to shut down. His family and friends were the reason his heart was beating. The only thing that actually kept him happy, determined and alive was the hope that the others were alive. He had not seen his family since his near-death experience. But that wasn't going to stop him, not after having gone this far. He had a serious purpose, and was determined to fulfil it.Only then would he die...

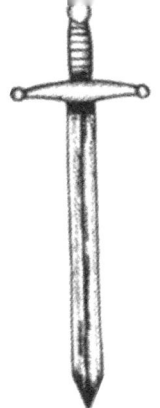

Voided

Nenthrate got up to find himself in the area where the war had taken place. He checked his surroundings. "Nobody?" he shrugged. OK! He called. *Now to solve why this sorcery keeps taking me to this specific place.It's like there's a clue here for sure! Well, I checked my surroundings, now let me check my pockets!* He checked his pockets to find the strange piece of paper that had led him to the first piece of the Ultimate Soul. It glowed like light. *Say—or think what??!* He realised that the paper was blank. Suddenly, the paper revealed a symbol. It looked like this:

It glowed for 10 – 15 seconds, then the paper suddenly ripped apart. As soon as the pieces touched the floor, they disappeared into thin air. He thought this was a sort of clue where the same symbol would be at his destination. *I have to search every inch of the planet,* thought Nenthrate. *I need a quick solution.* Immediately, he began to think of the probable shortcuts to the second fragment of the Ultimate soul. How would he reach there? It seemed almost impossible, but finally, he found a solution. The planet, (or whatever was bringing him here) was determined to send him to the same location, as if it wanted to show Nenthrate something, maybe even guide him! He realised at this moment that the Ultimate Soul was trying its best, perhaps desperately to lead Nenthrate to it. But then he realised this could be a trap. Which one should he have chosen?

He thought that this would have beens a lot easier with friends or family, but, at the same time, it appeared to be a near impossible task! Why??! he groaned. Then he realised that through the days, it was becoming increasingly quiet. In fact, it was too quiet. He looked around, expecting an attack. Nothing. He kept looking, but in the end, he decided it was just a waste of time. Then he looked at the bodies. Suddenly, a thought struck him. Maybe the bodies meant something. Maybe- Just then, he heard a rustle. Now he was starting to grow *really* suspicious. But nobody would be stupid enough to confront him when he was fully expecting it. Assuming that no one was there, Nenthrate resumed his search for the second fragment of the Ultimate soul.

He checked the bodies to see if there was anything unusual there, and he did find something! He shifted the body gently, and a passage appeared under it. This passage looked like a cave, but it had no traps and went on deeper. Nenthrate entered with a thousand questions in his mind- *Is this the reason The God of Evil chose to fight us specifically? To protect the Ultimate soul? Why did he divide it?*

A loud clang interrupted his thoughts and he looked up to see that the door above him had closed! This cave was a trap! Or was it? He felt something drop into his pocket. He did not believe his eyes. The same paper which had been magically torn apart was back! This time it showed a message; *Solve this riddle to escape, you have only one try to write down the solution!* Next, it showed the riddle: *What is all around us but invisible, indestructible and is a human's source of life?*

Nenthrate had a little trouble remembering what the humans had told him because of the fear that he would get it wrong. What was it? Ain? Aim? Air? Ah, that was it. Nenthrate sighed in relief but just when he was relaxing something fell into his pocket. Just then, he realised that he had not written the answer but he didn't have a pen or pencil. He nervously took out the mysterious object that had dropped in his pocket and to his great relief, it was a strange-looking pen with the same eye mark as the symbol that showed on the paper. He realised that this was no ordinary pen when he wrote with it. As soon as he was finished writing, the writing evaporated, the pen vanished and the paper disappeared and was replaced with a black and white compass that pointed north. Nenthrate concluded that the second fragment of the Ultimate Soul must be where the compass was pointing. He walked over the rocky, orangish-red surface of the gigantic planet, hoping that his destination would be waiting for him ahead. He used the compass as his only hope to get to the second fragment that would help destroy The God of Evil once and for all. He somehow had teleported out of the cavern and reached the surface of the planet. Finally, he reached an altar coated in flames. Nenthrate did not want to get burned but for a split second, the flames parted and he fleetingly saw the second shimmering fragment of the Ultimate Soul. He walked through the flames without getting burned as if by magic and lifted the fragment from its fiery prison. He ran away, hoping to never see this kind of strange altar again.

As he ran, he bumped into a group of people. His heart racing, he looked up to find Techno, Blados, and Gerados staring at him. He was so happy that it's nearly impossible to put it into words. He could just utter one word- "Guys." He was overjoyed to find them alive and well and enveloped them in a bear hug (I'm still trying to find the words to describe it for you).

He then noticed something glowing and very familiar in their hands Nenthrate was struck speechless and when he found his voice again, he managed to say- "How is this possible?! Are those actually the two missing pieces of the puzzle which I have been trying to put together single-handed with so much effort. To complete the picture, let me explain: those are the final two fragments of the Ultimate Soul, which was the source of The God of Evil's powers. When all four pieces are put together to make one whole and that is destroyed at one stroke, it would put an end to The God of Evil once and for all. "How in the True God's name did you get hold of these?" Blados started babbling but before he could say anything, Nenthrate said, "We *must* destroy them!" Blados continued his babbling- "So... what can I say, we escaped from our own ship and stumbled upon these. Quite ironic, isn't it?" Nenthrate sighed. "Here I was, thinking my job was dangerous and complicated enough but you must have had to go through a lot too. Blados looked at him and said, "I was about to say just that!" Blados considered this a coincidence. "Hold on," said Blados. Let me tell you the whole story...

"I was struggling to survive in the prison room. It was dark and it was very hard to communicate with each other, since we were locked in different prison cells. I was not surprised when we all were thinking of the same, near-impossible feat we wanted to achieve- escape. It was a perfect square how big exactly, I'm not sure. I wouldn't have spent my time measuring a prison, would I?" Blados paused for breath in that time, Nenthrate let out an amused laugh. Blados continued with his story. "Man, how the place smelled! That certainly increased our willpower to escape." "And destroy The God of Evil," added Gerados. "Right. We knew the ship like the back of our hand so he we broke our chains and went into the ventilation system. We eventually ran into each other and started to work together. After exiting the vents into the control room, we tried to fix up the ship but had to hide before the repairs were done, because the guards came in and we did not want to stick there much longer after that. We tried to eliminate all proof of our escape by not changing a single thing in the prison cells. Just when we reached the Emergency Exit, the alarm sounded and the ship went on full lockdown. We should not have fixed the systems. However, we were already outside. I've never seen the ship so heavily guarded. We were having trouble surviving on what food we had. Nenthrate said, speaking of food, I have not had any in 2 days. Blados ignored him and continued- We found a fragment of the Ultimate Soul but did not know what it was at that time. But it's unique colour and aura had us spellbound and we just had to carry it along. Same with the second fragment. We came upon it by chance and picked it up for that also seemed like a treasure which could not be left behind. Now we see how valuable these two things truly were." "I know," Nenthrate said. "Imagine if you had left them behind."

Nenthrate, in turn told them about Arsicon, how he got to know about the Ultimate Soul, coming face to face with a battle - weary God of Evil, being stuck in a cave and searching all over for the fragments of the Ultimate Soul. "Woah," said Blados. Now we've put the whole story together. Gerados looked at Nenthrate like *Now that we've put it together, it's time to take it apart again.* Nenthrate didn't know how to carry out the destruction of The Ultimate Soul, so he said, "We will have to keep it for a while." Blados looked a little scared, but he didn't say a word. He just shrugged and took a small step forward.

Nenthrate felt tired, and so hungry! Blados understood and took out some food out of a bag which was made out of a crushed vent chunk. Nenthrate decided not to tell him how weird it was- he tried to think how useful it was at the moment. Techno, who had remained silent gave a yawn. Nenthrate said, "You three sleep, you've been through a lot. I'll stand guard." He tried his best to make cozy, comfy beds for them and made a small but efficient fire to keep them warm and stood guard with his sword ready. Blados and the others thanked him happily and even offered to stand guard instead of him, but Nenthrate assured them that he could do it. He also pointed out a very obvious fact. They all needed sleep badly. Sarparin smiled. This was the Nenthrate they knew. Always putting the lives of others before his.

With this exhilarating thought, Blados, Techno, Sarparin and Gerados went off to sleep. In the deadly night, it turned out there were still a lot of creatures that were ready to devour prey. They were quite silent so Nenthrate had to cleverly spot them to know that they were there. More than once, Nenthrate had to fight off the deadly monsters on the planet, trying his best to finish them off but one snake bit him, causing him to bleed furiously and the venom overwhelmed him to a point where he started getting paralysed but before that happened, he swiped off its neck in a clean stroke. The venom had overwhelmed him too much, as a result, his pain eased and he went into a fitful slumber. He would present a scary sight when all of them woke up in the morning. But there arose another great problem soon enough...

In the morning, his wound was fine and the others were up, surprised at the sheer size and numbers of bones that littered the horizon. "Man," Blados said. "You sure had a tough job." Nenthrate winced a little and Blados noticed. Nenthrate told him about the bite and when he finished, something did not feel right. A figure stood in front of the morning sun. The God of Evil...

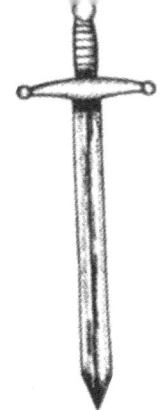

The final battle

Nenthrate looked deep into the blazing eyes of The God of Evil. This was the day that would end this, for Nenthrate or The God of Evil. He was not surprised or nervous. He had steely focus. He was ready. For years, he'd been preparing for this, and now he had a chance to show that he was the one destined to destroy The God of Evil once and for all. He took a deep breath and unsheathed his sword, the sword that would be drenched in The God of Evil's blood. But something was different about The God of Evil. Even though he tried to look smug, there was a slight hint of fear in his eyes. Nenthrate had never

The final battle

seen that before. Maybe it was because the Ultimate Soul was in their power. Seeing Nenthrate bare his sword, he unsheathed his blade. Nenthrate gave the Ultimate Soul to Blados and ran forward. It was a fierce fight, with swords clanging and blood dripping, but in the end, both were equally matched. Then, The God of Evil took one look at the Ultimate Soul and drove his blade into Nenthrate's heart. Nenthrate screamed and stumbled back. Clutching his heart to reduce the flow of the blood, he continued fighting. *Amazing...* The God of Evil thought. *Most people would be dead by now.* While The God of Evil was distracted, Nenthrate managed to snatch The God of Evil's blade and broke it in half with his own. The God of Evil was now vulnerable. Nenthrate took one last look at him, took the Ultimate Soul and broke it by slamming it on the ground. The explosion that took place was deafeningly devastating and before anyone knew it, the planet exploded and what was left of it stayed in space.

The God of Evil was lying on the ground, a pool of blood expanding around him. In his final breaths, he took Nenthrate's sword and stabbed him. Then, he closed his eyes, his last breath rattling in his chest. Techno and the others survived but didn't know what to feel. The God of Evil was dead, and Nenthrate was dying. They did not know how to save him. Would Nenthrate finally die? Was his purpose in life finally over? At first, they thought it was a befitting sacrifice by Nenthrate, their hero and a harbinger of hope for the future generations. One that would ultimately result in the prevalence of the greater good. The mission of Nenthrate's life was accomplished at last. He had fulfilled the vow that he had made not only to the Multiverse at large, but to himself too. Good had emerged victorious while Evil had been blown to smithereens.

The others had no time to process all that had happened before Nenthrate weakly called out to them. They rushed to his side. Nenthrate was barely alive, his own sword stuck in his chest, but he assured them he was fine. Luckily, just at that moment, a ship arrived with Radrason on it. Radrason took one look at Nenthrate and took him to the Medbay immediately. He would live to fight another day. But there was another question. Where were his mother, father and Snitchel? Alas, that is a mystery for another day...

The final battle

That was one facet of 'his' plan. 'He' would show himself to Nenthrate and do what 'his' pawn could not. Nenthrate's fate was directed by 'him...'

*How did Monster – **NENTHRATE** become a reality?*
*Where had Nenthrate's **Mom, Dad** and of course Snitchel gone?*
*Who made the **TELNATRAN** Fortress?*
And most importantly, Why?
*Discover more in the **UPCOMING BOOK**...*

NENTHRATE AND THE TELNATRAN FORTRESS

www.ingramcontent.com/pod-product-compliance
Lightning Source LLC
LaVergne TN
LVHW061553070526
838199LV00077B/7024